THE *Blackwell* COLLECTION

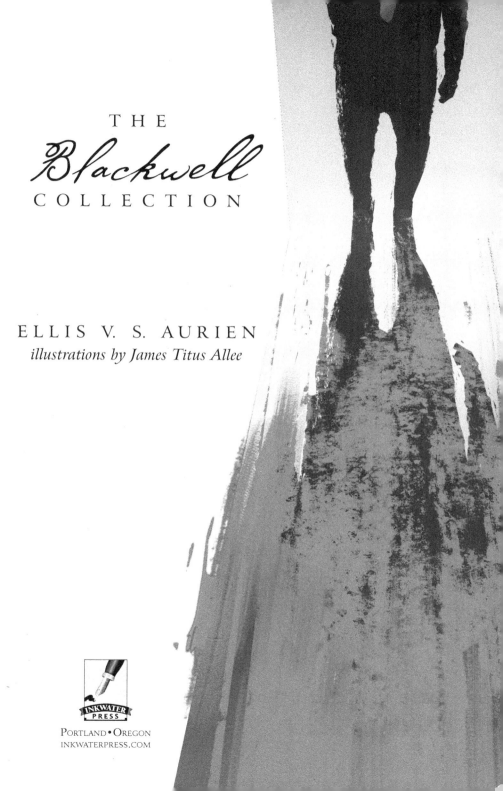

THE
Blackwell
COLLECTION

ELLIS V. S. AURIEN
illustrations by James Titus Allee

INKWATER
PRESS

PORTLAND • OREGON
INKWATERPRESS.COM

Publisher: Inkwater Press | www.inkwaterpress.com

Paperback   ISBN-13 978-1-62901-666-5 | ISBN-10 1-62901-666-7
Kindle   ISBN-13 978-1-62901-673-3 | ISBN-10 1-62901-673-X

1 3 5 7 9 10 8 6 4 2

Dedicated to those who have helped me find a faint, yet ever-present light in an overwhelming darkness.

CONTENTS

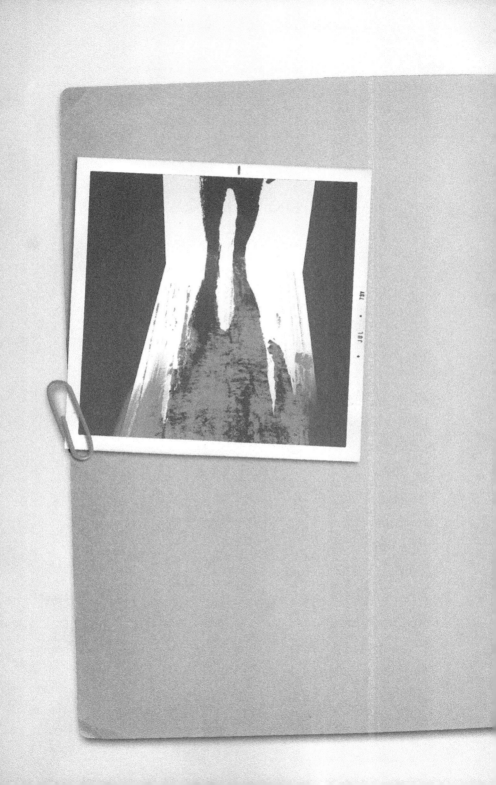

A Foreword from Professor Thomas H. Blackwell

NEVER HAVE I DESIRED, in the least, to seek the occult knowledge that I have learned over the course of my life.

Rather, it has found me. Time and time again, I have sensed the whispers and shadows of an archaic world far from our own. Through my tenure as the Chair of the History Department for the University of Ramsay, these tales came to me, showing me a faint glimmer of a darkness that dwells just beyond sight. After much deliberation, I would like to share what I have found, if only out of morbid curiosity as to what will result from releasing this collection to the public at large.

I have examined these documents more times than I care to admit, and I have yet to make any sense of them. For this reason, I have chosen to make this collection public with the hope that someone with knowledge far more dark and depraved than my own can find a meaning in all of this madness. I gave up on finding one for myself long ago, and I have accepted that I may never know why I was chosen to bear witness to these writings.

However, there is a fear that has welled in me since my collection began—a fear that has only grown. I am probably not in any immediate danger, but I am certain that there is something more to all of this. Hopefully the dread that I have faced will be subdued by the knowledge that I am no longer the lone soul in possession of these tales. But I doubt it will.

There is no greater solace, nor horror, than knowing that madness, in itself, is a primal mechanism for coping with the unexplainable. With this in mind, please heed my warning: What lies ahead may have no explanation, and the madness contained within may be far, far more than the simple words of tormented souls.

This document was delivered to me by a colleague who had attended an anthropological study in a small eastern country. This is apparently the well-known account of a local in the area. My colleague says that after they were told this tale, they cut their study short by a few weeks.

THE TOMB OF KAZIL-KORATH

THERE ARE CERTAIN THINGS that exist in this world—things that should not be present in the most disturbed thoughts of a deeply tormented soul. Things that cannot be explained simply because mortal science has no basis to acknowledge them. Things that have no right or reason to be.

These things lay purposefully forgotten by the wise ancestors of an unknowing populace, or were forcefully extinguished from the very fabric of time. They existed only as a barrier between our world and its predecessor—a plane of timeless waste and merciless barbarism, on a cosmic level far from any that I dare imagine.

A sole reminder of these ancient monstrosities is still known by the mortals who exist within its mercy—a lone reminder of a world that existed in a savage, godless time before the dawn of man: The Tomb of Kazil-Korath. This is an ancient, timeless ruin in this world's most desolate stretch of desert. The terrifying structure haunts the horizon for miles, striking dismay into the hearts of any who witness it across the sands that attempt, in vain, to conceal it.

Part of the horror that is inherently perpetuated by that place is due to the hushed tales of local tribes. These tribes, rumored to have existed in this basin for millennia beyond popular comprehension, all fear the site, yet offer no explanation for their dread other than antiquated stories and grim superstition.

Estimates of when the ruin was complete and functional have changed from generation to generation. Some say it was centuries before the first tribe settled in the valley. Some say it was uncountable ages before man first set foot in this world.

The only thing the tribes have unanimously agreed upon is decidedly unsettling: the tomb is a prison that holds a being known as Kazil-Korath, the "World Eater."

This entity stands accused of mercilessly destroying anything and everything that stood in its path, swallowing cities whole and leaving wakes of death and slaughter wherever it travelled. Nobody knows exactly how or whom it was captured by—only that it was banished to the tomb and sealed within, with magic so vile that all records of it were purged alongside the beast.

This story, documented by time-warped scripture and rudimentary hieroglyphs, was left behind by unknown scribes to detail the struggle and sacrifice of countless prehistoric beings who selflessly ensured the monstrosity remain forever pacified.

The stories seemed unbelievable, but their consistent dread had been enough to keep most from investigating further. Most who were foolish enough to try and disturb the ruins were either never heard from again—or worse, confined to a madhouse for the rest of their short days.

Every last one of those unlucky few spoke of horrible,

depraved findings inside the tomb. That was the most anyone dared recount. Any further questioning resulted in gibberish, or inarticulate sobs that alone spoke of the horrors the survivors had witnessed. This was what made even the bravest of adventurers decide to stay away.

However, not all of the men who found themselves face-to-face with the ruin met this fate. Of the few who returned with their sanity intact, the ones who spoke a word of their journey could be counted on one's fingers. Their survival, and the sanity they retained, seemed unforgivingly random.

One "recent" survivor had made his journey a little over forty years ago. He had investigated the disappearance of local village children, who had likely gone on an excursion to the tomb to give themselves a "harmless" scare. When the man returned, he never uttered a word of what he had seem, simply telling the elder of the village that the children were "gone" before packing his tent and disappearing into the starry, bleak night.

That man's recollection, mysterious as it was, was the only one that locals had directly experienced until I made my own ill-fated trip to the tomb. My journey had been far from voluntary or desired in any way. Instead, cruel and unjust fate had twisted plans for me.

On a blistering mid-August day, a pack of tribal bandits murdered my traveling companions after robbing us blind, taking everything but the clothes on my back. After taking their haul, they spared me, leaving me marooned in the infinite sands of the forsaken desert—a wicked joke to which I will never understand the punchline.

As a result of being left with no water, food, or protection from the sweltering heat, I found myself shambling toward anything that I could use as shelter—deciding after great deliberation that anything was better than dying slowly in the boil that surrounded me.

A sandstorm had been brewing for a few hours, but I could not have predicted its ferocity when it finally materialized. The dry desert air became addled with burning sand, tearing against my burned skin with a fury and pain that I could have scarcely imagined. My caution was replaced by desperation. I had only one option.

Throwing away all thought, doubt, reason, and common sense, I ventured toward the nearest sanctuary from the heat: the ruined tomb.

Convincing myself that I would not survive a trek to the nearest settlement, I decided I would only enter the tomb far enough to get shelter from the storm, and stay until nightfall. Then I'd make my way to the nearest town and move on from this horrid twist of fate. The plan was far from foolproof, but I knew it was the only chance I had.

With the determination of a man possessed, I began my trek, vowing that the death of my friends would not be forgotten and their attackers would see some form of justice—a vow that will forever remain unfulfilled.

Within minutes, I found myself staring at the massive, finely detailed walls of the tomb's entrance, intricately carved with calligraphic symbols and lost vocabulary. I was taken back by the outlandish beauty, though I lacked the faintest idea of what any of it meant.

It was hard to believe that something so wondrous had such a malevolent history, despite the overbearing eeriness it conveyed in its majesty. Still, I knew that if I remained exposed much longer, I would not survive. Taking one last look at the ancient arts around me, I begrudgingly lowered myself down the staircase, and found myself becoming enveloped by a growing darkness.

As it grew darker, it grew colder. Impossibly colder. Mere moments ago I had been burning alive, and now I was shivering violently. This planted yet another seed of fear in the back of my mind. But I pressed on, spurred by the boiling sands that were still somehow finding their way down the stairwell.

The moment I lost the feeling of sand brushing against my skin, I stopped dead in my tracks. I looked back, seeing a light implausibly far away—from both above and below. The uncomfortable and decrepit nature of the tomb was enough to make me feel as uncomfortable as physically possible. Still, I held myself in place, despite the overwhelming urge to retreat, knowing that staying here would mean certain death.

As the light below began to shimmer and seemed to shake in what I perceived to be a welcoming way, I felt my anxiety waver. It rose but simultaneously fell, in an odd but not entirely dreadful way.

I tried to take a better look. But something caught my attention first: The sound of something flowing, like water from a stream. Every fear dimmed under the promise of refreshment and continued survival, leading my body to slowly move toward the sound without my mind's consent, only listening to its primal instincts.

After a few steps, my mind returned, and I stopped in my tracks as the tales and dread once again became apparent. An internal conflict raged between primitive desire and rational thought. It was a risk, a sure trap, but my desires became overwhelming, urging me to press on, against the knowledge of the danger, and driven only by an overpowering thirst that had only recently become apparent.

As I walked toward the light, I found myself growing more and more unsettled. Time seemed to slow down, everything being drawn out much longer than it should have been, every step taking longer and longer as I went along.

As I got closer to the light, the sound became thicker—like waves crashing, but deeper. It sounded painful, with a haunting overtone of sentience growing more constant and voluminous as the distance slowly closed. But still, I persevered, despite the onset of paranoia—if only partially consenting to my body's movement.

As I continued through the cavern, the light became more prominent on the walls, revealing ghastly imagery in the form of paintings and etchings, all detailing gruesome scenes depicting a disgusting, worm-like monster violently destroying depicted civilizations with a gaping maw and reckless abandon.

It is here that my memories begin to shift and become as hazy as the very sands that sealed my fate. I recall that as I drew closer to the light, the paintings only got more deranged, violent, and sadistically detailed. Horror seeped into my veins in a way that I can only describe as painful.

I found myself unable to reason with my own body. I was the prisoner now, unable to stop. The sound had ceased to resemble anything fluid—it sounded like violent thrashings against something solid and rough.

By now I was over the edge of simple fear, waiting for the moment that I would reclaim control of myself and turn back into the storm. But that feeling simply never came. I could not reclaim control, no matter the effort. I simply watched the spectacle before me as my body continued without me.

After some time and a few more shaky steps, I found myself overlooking a ledge. Below was the most horrible, godless thing I could have imagined, and I found myself only able to stand and silently stare in pure awe of the monstrosity that outshone even the best of its ancestral depictions.

The creature's massive black body shimmered in the dim lighting—twisting and contorting at seemingly impossible angles, a movement accompanied by the sound of worn cartilage crackling. Dozens of sharp eyes dotted its long, fat form, all bloodshot and clouded. It seemed like it was in immense pain, wandering aimlessly along the winding passage it was in, stones grinding under it as it groaned loudly. Its groans caused the stone around me to rumble.

I was immobile, but aware—still paralyzed by fear and unable to fully understand what was now within a stone's throw of me. It took all my strength to take a deep breath in a desperate attempt to regain control. But when my body obliged, I immediately wished it hadn't.

The breath alerted the monster to my position, and it took quick action to seek me out. It slithered toward me, and I found myself completely immovable again as it flicked its eyes toward me in a gruesome fashion. No matter how hard I tried to move, act, or breathe, I couldn't. As the creature inched toward me, my desperation grew.

After an excruciating wait, I found myself face to face with this beast. I was now perched on the very edge of my sanity, staring into what must have been the primary eyes of the putrid creature, neither one of us daring to move.

It was first to act. It opened its mouth and let out a ferocious scream, loud enough to shake me to my very core. It continued until every sound around me drowned into nothingness, never to return. The resulting horror overtook me, sending me to the floor in sobs, pushing me to a point of duress I would not wish upon even the men who put me in this hell.

However, the worst realization came when I found that my pain was not the creature's goal. Between sobs, my vision flickered. I only caught glimpses of the horror that awaited me until I found enough clarity to understand that the terror was far from over.

What I saw was finally enough to throw me over the edge, where I regained control of my body for a precious few moments. With a scream, I sprang away from the beast, faster than I thought was possible.

All I can recall from that moment onward is running aimlessly from the godless depths of that tomb into the desert—just as burning and boundless as I had left it. I continued on into what I knew was a far more merciful death than any that awaited me below.

I was found a short time later by a citizen carrying supplies for trade along a common merchants' route. According to her, I was sobbing inconsolably about something I had seen, begging for her to let me die. She says I fought her attempts at salvation for some time before finally giving in to the exhaustion.

They call my survival a miracle, but I know otherwise.

What I saw that day will forever be embedded into the darkest depths of my mind. A constant fear that will never pass or wither with age. An undying rift in my sanity that will never be repaired.

The being I saw that day was unimaginable, unforgivable, and terrifying beyond my wildest dream. Yet it was not the worst thing I saw that dreaded day.

For I didn't just see the magnum opus of an embodied nightmare, undulating endlessly in a hell of mortal creation.

I saw thousands of them.

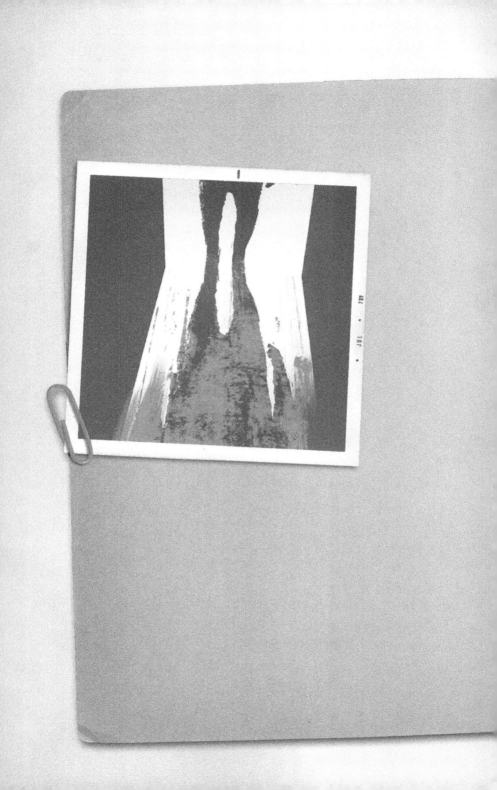

THIS NOTE WAS FOUND IN A RUINED HUNTING
SHED ON ONE OF THE LARGEST NATIVE
RESERVATIONS IN NORTHERN WASHINGTON, WITH
NO SIGN OF ITS AUTHOR. TO MY KNOWLEDGE,
NO INFORMATION HAS BEEN PROVIDED AS TO
THEIR CURRENT STATUS OR WHEREABOUTS.

MANIFEST DESTINY

I ONCE BELIEVED THAT there was nothing more terrifying than a life wasted in the dull thrum of a corporate machine. I feared that I was destined to fall victim to the fate that had claimed so many before me.

As the mocking voices of my dead friends resonate through the murky, blackened forest that entombs me, I now know how foolish I was to be scared of such a luxury. In my self-immolating spiral of boredom and selfish nihilism, I had never opened my eyes to the true horrors hiding just outside of common perception.

It was supposed to be a simple deer hunt—something to realign the dissatisfied minds of three childhood friends. With honest excitement, we jumped at the idea, synchronizing our schedules to allow an extended absence in the early autumn.

Our days were quickly filled with preparations. No expense was spared, and as the day drew near, we had a formidable stock of everything we needed, and more. Food, tools, packs, and rifles were as carefully chosen as the location of our hunt: Pat, who was of Native American descent, had negotiated with members of his father's tribe to allow us to access the forest that graced their lands. However, he eventually let slip that Julian and I were never mentioned in their deal.

The revelation did nothing to lessen our enthusiasm. As the day arrived, we were ready to venture into the unknown—three invincible men standing tall in the face of their perceived chains.

We were wrong. So incredibly wrong.

Upon our entry, we were awestruck by the beauty of the untamed wilderness—vast and mighty even by the standards of Washington State. Pat mouthed a quick prayer with a toothy grin, and Julian and I were simply astonished by nature's irrepressible beauty.

Our first night was uneventful, but very pleasant. After the fire had been stoked, Julian revealed that he had brought a bottle of whisky, and we quickly set upon it. We stayed up far later than we had planned, swapping stories and laughter between sips from the bottle.

By the time we woke, day had long since arrived. My eyes adjusted slowly to the light, bringing my attention to a dull headache and a strange sight: Pat standing outside the tent, lingering quietly despite the morning chill. Julian had woken slightly before me. He spoke first, startling Pat. When questioned, Pat simply stated that we needed to move deeper, as he had an odd feeling about the area.

We obliged quickly, but I caught Pat as he attempted to pocket what appeared to be a small, carefully-carved wooden totem. Before I could query his intentions, he made eye contact and shook his head. I decided not to say anything. We quickly packed our camp, extinguished the few remaining embers, and continued on our journey.

Just before nightfall, we found an ideal clearing a short way from the main trail. We dug a pit for a fire and followed quickly with the tent. By night, we again had a strong fire going. We were warm and happy, and the events of the morning had passed from our minds. We shared more stories of life, and gripes about work, and we deepened our bond of brotherhood over an evening of much-needed peace.

By morning, our tranquility was gone. A tension filled the air as we awoke again to see Pat outside the tent, mumbling to himself. He paced nervously around the tent, and I spared no time in joining him outside. I quickly saw what had shaken him.

Any semblance of our camp was gone. The remains of the campfire and our gear were nowhere to be found, and nothing looked even remotely familiar. I realized Pat was chanting something quietly, no longer attempting to hide his artifact from us. I recognized the figure from our childhood. It was an effigy, a small totem featuring the likenesses of a deer, a bear, and a fox, carved with care into a palm-sized piece of oak wood. Larger, more ornate versions of the same totem had been displayed in Pat's home, and in those of his relatives. I remembered his father telling me that it had been a symbol of protection in times of need. I knew Pat had been raised to understand the traditions of his family, but had never seen him actively engage with their beliefs before now. When I tried to speak to him, he hushed me. He continued his chant as Julian joined me in standing awestruck again, this time in bewilderment and fear.

Upon the end of the frantic chant, Pat wasted no time in ordering us to pack the tent and move with him. He hurriedly explained that the forest was not as large as it seemed, and no matter the situation, we would find our way out. He further explained that these things happened on occasion in these woods, citing ancestral tales of their harmless trickery.

He may have fooled Julian, but I remained doubtful. As Julian occupied himself with the breakdown of the tent, I quietly demanded a real explanation. At first, Pat tried to reinforce his claims, but quickly realized the futility of lying to me.

For a moment, his facade of steely command slipped into panic as he whispered, "Something evil is near."

With that, I was moved. I assisted Julian, knowing that this was no foolish trick. The horror in my friend's eyes spoke far more than his words, and we soon departed. My father once told me that to panic in the woods was a death sentence—common sense and thoughtfulness were greater tools than any physical charm.

However, I could not help but silently unravel as the woods grew less and less familiar. Pat reassured us, but never lost contact with the totem in his hands. As the night began to fall again, we reluctantly set the tent up once more, this time hidden under a small overhang. We kept our rifles close and resolved to sleep in shifts.

Halfway through the night, I awoke to the sound of a faint crunching of leaves. The moonlight illuminated two silhouettes—one of my friend, another of what seemed to be a small animal. The animal seemed injured, slinking along the outside of the tent. Whoever was standing guard turned to the silhouette before screaming. As he drew his rifle, I felt my other companion jolt awake. We watched as the animal rose on its hind legs, defying its previous size to stand a head taller than our companion outside. It loosed a foul, watery gurgle as its broken antlers blotted the moonlight above. The animal's form stepped closer to the tent, casting my friend completely in shadow.

A soft prayer began next to me as my heart began to sink. I turned to see Pat, eyes filled with tears, clutching his totem as the creature bore down on what I now knew was Julian. His rifle fired, but did nothing to stop the vicious onslaught. The tent shook as the creature screamed a half-animal, half-human cry, narrowly overlapping with Julian's screams of agony. Blood splattered the tent as the screams lost volume. I grabbed for my rifle but was intercepted by Pat, who forced me to the ground and cupped his hand over my mouth, silencing my hyperventilation. I felt tears on my cheek as the creature stood again, its form more massive and mangled than before. At the sound of something large being dragged away, an eerie calm washed over us. We both fought to stay awake as the sound dissipated, leaving only the whispers of the trees and the rhythmic chirping of the bugs in its wake.

I do not know how long it took for the powerful sleep to overtake us, but I will never forget the terror in my heart as I awoke. Once again, Pat had woken before me, but this time he was not standing, or moving. This time he lay just outside the open tent flap, weeping to himself.

As I exited, I realized why he had taken this form. The tree line was familiar, but not in a way that soothed me. Rather, dread overtook my senses as I realized that we were in the same location as the previous morning. Our previous day's journey had been in vain.

I half-heartedly shook Pat, empathizing with his hopelessness. He responded by shivering, and he spat a few unkind words as the morning chill met us. I assisted him, pulling him to his feet as we resolved to silently move again, this time opposite the path of the previous night.

Pat constantly mumbled to himself, seemingly unaware of my presence. A few times he looked to me, eyes full of regret and guilt, before moving his gaze back to the path ahead. As the trail began to fork, we pondered our next move.

I remember feeling a warm sensation on my scalp just before Pat looked up. His guttural scream shook me to the core, chasing any semblance of serenity from my mind as my vision blurred. Above us was Julian—or rather, what had once been Julian. His entrails hung down, torn asunder by something I could only assume was incredibly strong, vicious, and merciless. His pale face was stuck in an expression of sheer dread and immense pain, hands still frozen in a defensive posture. I felt sick, but Pat shoved me before I could oblige my instincts to be sick.

I looked up to see nearby branches rustling. Pat shoved me again as an impossibly warped antler broke the tree line, throwing us both into a frenzied sprint. As we ran, an acrid scent of blood and rot filled the air. The branches around us began to thin, and we suddenly found ourselves tumbling down a steep slope, unable to slow ourselves as we plummeted onto a dark plateau.

As we came to a stop, my heart seemed to follow. Pain shot through my body as I began to take in the ghastly sight of what now surrounded us. All around were bones— some animal, some human. All were broken, cracked, and scraped clean of anything living. The monumental decay was potent and visceral, and we were paralyzed in the face of what awaited us.

I tried to speak, but my throat seized as something slammed into the ground next to us. We sheepishly looked and wished we had not. On the ground, somehow more broken than before, was Julian. Pat could no longer hold back hysteria as I silently collapsed into myself. We were being hunted, and the malevolent irony was not lost on me.

I do not know how long it took for us to once again become mobile. All I know is that the night followed far too quickly, enshrouding us once again. We silently followed the edge of the plateau back into the colossal woods, this time not knowing any path or having any true destination in mind. We merely shambled on, reminiscent of lambs to the slaughter.

It came when the moon reached its peak. Julian's voice broke over the forest and pleaded for salvation. We hunched behind a large boulder as the voice continued, its throaty croak piercing the stone that hid us. I raised my rifle, moving from my cover momentarily to see what awaited us.

It was a deer, but not like any I had ever seen. Its ribs were exposed, and its head was bent at an impossible angle at the neck, with each of its legs awkwardly protruding from its lanky body. Julian's voice rang from its lips again, begging for help, and I fixed my sights. I fired, blowing chunks of its midsection away. It fell, but Pat was now almost inconsolable. He grabbed me and pushed me away from the stone. He followed, urging me to flee with him.

I turned to see why, and quickly realized my mistake. While the deer had been stunned, the loss of what had once been its heart did little to stop it. I raised my rifle to fire again, but fear overtook that impulse. It rose on its hind legs again, bones shivering and cracking as its mottled coat began to tear and stretch to make room for its quickly expanding, patchy flesh. Its body widened and shook as its forelegs grew long and clawed, cold veins protruding from its thin flesh. Its head became semi-human, still broken at the impossible angle, with the warped antlers still tearing through its greying skin. As the form grew massive, I could no longer stomach it. I turned to Pat, and we began to flee through the darkness. The mocking tone of what once had been Julian's voice cried out a few moments after our departure, signaling what I guessed was the completion of the creature's transformation. Every few moments afterward, a booming roar sounded, growing nearer and nearer with each of its colossal steps.

I could feel the vibrations of its steps only moments later, and could hear its labored breath closing in. As a cool breeze met the back of my neck, I felt my body tense. Pat tackled me as the creature swiped at my back, sending us both down a hill into a thick brush.

The creature looked around, this time roaring with its own abysmal cry. Pat's eyes were frantic. He knew the end was near, and he knew that this hideaway was only temporary. He looked to me once, choking a cry, before handing his totem to me. He whispered, "It'll all be all right," between sobs. I wanted to ask what he meant, but before I could choke a word out, he stood and screamed, running away from the creature and I.

The creature's neck snapped toward my friend, and it quickly fell to its forelegs before giving chase. As Pat and the creature disappeared over a ridge, I fled the opposite direction.

Every broken branch brought me one step closer to the edge—one step closer to collapsing under monumental anxiety. A scream broke over the night once more, and I could not tell its origin.

As my legs felt ready to give, something caught my eye—the tent we had left behind, drooping with wear but otherwise still intact. I thought for a moment, before climbing under it.

As the emotions of the night mixed with the claustrophobia, I became inconsolable. As the ground around me began to shake, I contemplated the necessity or effectiveness of my sanctuary. However, as Pat's voice rang across the night, just as broken and soulless as Julian's, I realized I had to survive.

I crawled and huddled against the bottom of the structure, trying my hardest to ignore the shadows of antlers that danced across the fabric of my prison. I remained as small and still as possible. A familiar foul wind crossed my neck as the creature grunted, now impossibly close.

"It'll all be all right," a familiar voice croaked, causing me to close my eyes tightly. Each second, my emotions became harder to contain. Suddenly, the tent above me shook violently as the creature laughed, tearing the top of the tent asunder. Yet I remained hidden, just below certain death.

After a long time and much mental torture, I sensed I was alone again.

In the wee hours of the morning, I realized how truly alone I was. I looked from my perch to see nothingness in all directions. Blood streaks covered the area around the tent, with random chunks of flesh dotting the ground where that monster had once stood.

I travelled aimlessly after this point, in search of any salvation, or at least something to forestall my fate. I heard constant whispers in the trees. Every few minutes, I heard them again, watching, waiting.

I haven't seen the beast since its pursuit, but I can feel it near.

By strange circumstance, I have found a small shed, which has proven to be an adequate, if temporary, shelter. There is nothing in here for my use, save for a few rusted blades and some assorted tools, but it offers me a temporary reprieve from the open woods. It is here that I found this stationary, and here where I shall document what may be my final hours. I have kept quiet as the night has passed, using this log to keep me focused and grounded. I have heard something just beyond the door on multiple occasions, but have no way nor desire to ascertain its origin—save for opening the door and exposing myself to whatever danger is there.

I know that I cannot wait much longer. Escape is my only chance, and every moment I waste makes that chance grow slimmer. My eyes fight off fatigue, and my stomach rumbles with hunger. But I'm prepared. I know my rifle will not work, and I know there is no simple tool that will save me from this hell. The only thing I am taking when I flee, save for the clothing on my back, is Pat's totem. It took the three of us two days to make it here, but something deep within me assures me I have a fighting chance alone. Upon full light, I shall make my escape.

If you find this note, do not search any further. The end has come, and the only thing left to be found, aside from a pile of nameless gore and unmatched horror, is something that must remain lost at any cost.

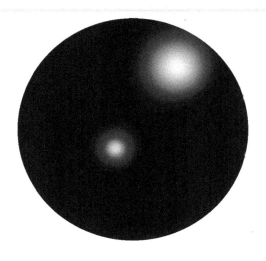

This statement began as an editorial sent anonymously to various newspapers across the southwestern states. The topic had long since been a focal point for conspiracy theorists and the like, but this paper sowed further questioning. To this day, the events that occurred in Raro, Arizona have no satisfying explanation.

THE CURIOUS FATE THAT BEFELL RARO, ARIZONA

THE DEVIL'S GREATEST TRICK was

not convincing the world that he does not exist. No, his greatest trick was to convince us that curiosity was not of his design.

We collectively have the inability to leave well enough alone. Some view this as a motivation and asset, but the few who gaze beyond the veil know better.

When the colors first began to blot the sun from the warm Arizona sky, I was there. From the beginning of the madness, I watched cautiously.

The rural villa became a tourist haven overnight. With the scientists came the skeptics. The philosophers were not far behind. As the colors began to shimmer over the once-quiet town, the bohemians arrived. By the time the scientists had declared their studies fruitless and the phenomenon unexplainable, word had spread beyond the sea.

I refused to align with any of the masses. I stood in condemnation of the newcomers. It was obvious that whatever this was, it was not right.

As the colors became vibrant sparks across the night sky, I observed the madness below. Though the event was isolated to the skies over the town, the masses became uneasy. Fear pulsated through the crowds, and speculation arose with it. Doomsayers and evangelists clashed as if they were armed to their rotting teeth with divine truth, while bohemians and philosophers were overtaken by the hedonism of the mystic unknown.

I knew better. As the colors aligned, forming a thunderous Technicolor mass, the chaos overtook the tourists. It sent the masses into a writhing heap of despair and rage. Words became screams, terror reigned free, and wonder became panic.

I continued observing from my hidden vantage, refusing to give in to the temptations of paranoia that clawed at my veins. As the mass above congealed into a solid form, a moment of peace fell upon the tumultuous town. The mob reflected, if only for a moment. Hands were joined. Screams became sobs. All at once, there was understanding.

The form flashed once, and the crowd gasped. At once, the object crashed to the earth, colliding with a small home on the outskirts of the town. Though unscathed, the crowds seemed immovable. After minutes of uncertainty, one brave, foolish soul moved to the object.

I moved closer, sheepishly. I refused to approach the crowd, but stood within view of what was about to occur. The first fellow entered the ruins of the home, pushing into the unknown with a show of false bravery. After a few long moments, he re-emerged with a confused look.

"It's a mirror!" he cried, as a similar look crossed over the crowd. "It's just a mirror!"

Quickly, many people huddled around it. The broken house overflowed with the gawking masses, and more attempted to push inward.

Despite numerous prods and pokes, the mirror gained no smudge. Despite bashing and aggression, it refused to crack. Some praised the mirror, reveling in its possible divinity. Others grew disappointed and left. Some, like me, kept their distance, for something told us there was more coming.

We were right. Nobody remembers the identity of the curious soul who caused that to happen. But one individual asked a question—a simple question, directed to the mirror itself.

"Where do you come from?" the patron asked, simply speaking aloud. His curiosity turned to wonder and then horror when the mirror's reflection spun into a tempest of stars and veils, shooting far beyond any familiar cosmos toward a galaxy of mystic lights and swirling nebulae. The crowd gasped. They all leaned close, packing the ruined house even farther beyond its capacity. They were completely and utterly mystified.

When the portent swirled back to the reflection of the wide-eyed mob, a host of questions and queries flooded the silence of the night. People begged and fought to get closer to the mirror, spilling blood and ravenously moving closer toward the clairvoyant that awaited them.

Quickly, the mirror established its rules by way of trial and error. All beings were limited to a single question, with all others being ignored. One question could be asked at a time, with no filter of common decency. The mirror was as graphic and crude as the questions it was asked, with no question being too much or too little.

Love was tested, greed was fed, wonder was sated, and life's greatest mysteries were quickly and mercilessly debunked. I for one truly believed that the denizens of

Raro, still multiplying in number as the news continued to spread, had gone too far. By the time my cautiousness was malevolently rewarded, nothing was sacred.

The hysteria ended as it had begun: with a simple question.

One foolish soul, upon reaching the head of the line, sheepishly muttered one simple phrase: "How is this ... all of this ... going to end?"

Within moments, a panic fell over the crowd. Screams once again echoed through the night and countless men and women fled the horror. The foolish soul who asked the question and many who were near him fell to the ground, screaming in agony. Braver souls attempted in vain to destroy the mirror, but when their eyes met it, they were not spared the fate of their predecessors. After what had seemed like an eternity of macabre terror, the mirror's image gave way to its resting self—unfeeling as to the atrocity it had just committed.

When the damage was done, dozens were lost. The lucky ones died of sheer fright, but the ones who were stronger met a far worse fate: they were enslaved to the horrors within their minds, unable to process the terror they had witnessed.

Overnight, the government men arrived. They had no badges or credentials, but were organized and efficient. They cordoned the alien object off and spared no quarter to those who attempted to approach. Bags of concrete were delivered to the guards, and preparations for a hushed operation began as survivors of the mirror's visions were shepherded away, awaiting a fate that I refuse to dwell upon.

Unfortunately, I was no longer immune to the

curiosity of my peers. I may be wiser than some, but I am far from perfect. Words cackled across my brain, begging me to ask one last question. In my mind I knew what it was to be, and my desire overtook my reason.

I memorized the guard's patterns, quickly. They did little to protect the mirror, and I felt that this was because they feared it. In a way, I felt bad for the mirror. I doubted it was conscious, and more, I doubted that it meant any malevolence. It was a misunderstood, abused object that had found the wrong home.

As I began to sneak into the newly constructed fortress, whispers did as well. The men were scared of the mirror. They wanted to destroy or move it, but lacked the strength. They resolved only to bury it and pray no foolish soul would dare reawaken the all-knowing terror that would surely be waiting.

While I was glad they wanted to bury it, I felt that I had earned my chance. I had earned this question. I was not going to give up that easily.

After a few more moments of sneaking about, I found myself alone with the mirror. It was large—much larger than I had assumed. It stood above me, grandiose and opulent, existing without frame or borders. A sense of dread loomed with it, but I knew why I had come. I had to be brave.

I stuttered a moment before finding the exact words.

"What can we do to save ourselves from the end?" I asked, gently.

As the mirror began to fill with color and swirl together, my heart sank and I regretted my prodding. But I was in too far to back out now.

The colors mixed into something far beyond what I

could imagine. It became a form, a void—something tangible but nonexistent. Winds swirled past me as the vision faded, opening a door beyond mortal comprehension.

As the winds dragged me toward the unknown, I attempted to scream, but was met with silence. As my eyes opened, my mind followed. I was alone, far deeper in the void than I desired or could imagine. And yet, the vision did not cease.

Every sense fell away as my mind connected the metaphorical dots. My very soul began to ache as I realized just what the prophet was telling me. It was clear—far too clear.

When the harrowing vision ended, I escaped into the night—far beyond the mirror, which was now irretrievably sealed by government men in a concrete bunker far below the ground.

Authorities provided a scientific explanation as to the nature of the artifact, and that explanation quickly became a folk legend. The proposed explanation spoke of vapors from space, comets, atmospheric conditions, and natural elements combining to create a state of mass psychosis and hallucination—more than enough for those who wished to forget what they had experienced.

I am one of the only ones who knows the truth ... the only one who knows the nature of the beyond ... and the only one to know the hopelessness that awaits.

For when I gazed into the veil and asked my question, knowing full well in my heart that I already knew the answer, it answered with nothing.

Absolute nothingness.

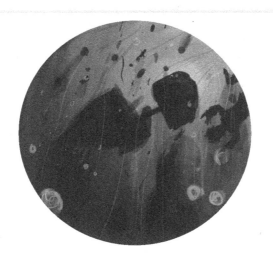

THIS ENTRY COMES FROM THE PERSONAL
JOURNAL OF MY GREAT-GRANDFATHER, AND
IS ONE OF THE MAIN REASONS I CHOSE TO
BECOME A HISTORIAN. IT WAS THE FIRST STORY
IN MY COLLECTION, AS WELL AS MY ENTRY IN TO
THE STRANGE WORLD I NOW FIND MYSELF IN.

THE SIREN

POSEIDON AND I HAD been well-acquainted
for many years before I found myself begging for his forgiveness and mercy. With every storm, every ounce of
cannon fire, every loose flame, I found myself saying a
quick prayer to the ocean's guardians, hoping that they
would protect me on my travels. But this time, my prayers
went unanswered.

The cold embrace of the sea was oddly more painful
than the blast that tossed me overboard. The bailing
bucket I had been holding had somehow found its way
under me, and was barely holding my unresponsive mass
above the waves. My comrades were too busy trying to
save the ship to assist me, but they knew I was in trouble.
Their screams gently began to lose volume as the bucket
slipped out from under me, and I sank beneath the waves.

As I descended lower into the darkness that was a
source of both dread and wonder, I found myself at peace
with my inability to act. My body turned to the surface,
giving me a strangely clear view of a quickly fading world
above me. I truly thought I had perished, until I felt the
last breath of an earth seemingly left behind exit my lungs.

I felt a strange harmony as the light faded, both liter-ally and metaphorically. The sea's embrace quickly turned from an icy grip to a loose, warm descent into my own demise. It was both obscene and strangely poetic. As mem-ories of my life flashed through my mind, I had a curious sensation. I found myself no longer gently descending, but being pulled toward the depths.

I realized then that I was no longer alone. The light slipped into a comforting darkness as I felt hands turn my body away from the surface and toward the unknown. The pressure building inside my skull mixed with the small bubbles of air escaping my lungs created a symphony that highlighted the hopelessness of my encroaching fate. As the pressure became unbearable, a soothing voice crept into my mind.

"Shh," it said. "Let your mind wander and your body rest."

I was in no position to argue with what was likely my unraveling mind, so I obeyed. Suddenly, a dim light appeared in my fading vision, and as something crept across my lips, I felt relief. My lungs came back to life as I realized that I was no longer dying. The moment of unsure anxiety faded as the light grew brighter. As I drifted toward it, I remembered all the old stories I'd heard about this moment of serenity. I had always thought it to be an old wives' tale, but now I found myself basking in the glow.

As the light grew brighter, I began to notice the fea-tures of its creator. It was a creature reminiscent of woman clad in a flowing dress—but only to a certain degree. Her skin was as green as the kelp that surrounded her, and her hair was fluorescent with the lights of the far north. Her eyes were pale, and her smile radiant. As I approached her, I noticed that, rather than a true dress, she was surrounded by various deep-sea creatures. The sight justified every sense of wanderlust I had ever felt.

I realized now that the air in my lungs was being supplied by one of her long, porous arms. As my eyes slowly regained their focus, I realized that her hand was placed over my mouth. I smiled at the irony. She beckoned me closer, and I found myself regaining strength. I swam with all my might toward her, rapidly closing in on her beauty.

But something did not feel right. It all seemed rehearsed. Regardless of the old wives' tales I had heard about a peaceful death, years on the sea had taught me that anything this perfect couldn't be true. My mind raced as I realized that I was no longer swimming, but being dragged toward the being. The creatures that made up her dress swam around her, occasionally revealing that underneath her garment was nothing but a mass of tentacles leading somewhere below. As my eyes met hers, I found myself forced to look beyond the beauty.

As soon as I did, my heart sank. I didn't see the paradise I expected—far from it. I saw a field of greying bodies swaying with the currents, all bound by the feet with the same mass that surrounded my face. Their bulging eyes glowed against the light of the being, all pleading and begging for mercy. The pressure wracked their bodies with every movement, sending agony across their mangled forms. In my horror, I almost hadn't noticed that not only were they deprived of the creature's air, but they were now silently screaming—their broken mouths agape.

I kicked and fought against the creature's arm in vain as I found myself in a full panic. I was determined not to let this creature imprison me, but I could not escape its grasp. I found myself on the verge of tears as I looked back into her eyes, which were no longer a beam of hope but rather a soulless void of pure nothingness.

Her smile turned into a look of vicious hunger, and I found myself giving up hope. As I felt something begin to wrap around my foot, I cast another sidelong prayer to the sea's gods—this time not for mercy, but for power.

In this moment of darkness came a revelation. The blade I had kept to ward off my greedy companions dug into my ankle as I realized my escape was not impossible. In a swift motion, I dug my hand into my boot and drew my knife, swinging wildly at the creature's arm. The blade connected and the creature let out an impossible shriek. As her grasp broke, so did the connection to the air she supplied me. The icy rush hit me with the force of a thousand cannons as the last of the air escaped my lungs. But the determination in my heart allowed me to push past the pain. My foot slipped from the noose surrounding it and I wildly thrust myself to the surface.

The creature's screams of pain turned into a bloodcurdling yell of fury as the currents changed in my favor. I paddled with the strength of a man greater than myself. Despite the primal fear in my heart, I attempted to ignore the desolation that coursed through my body.

A few moments of blind struggle passed before I found myself gazing at the light of the surface world. It seemed closer now than ever before, drawing me on as writhing tentacles clouded my view. But I had come too far to let myself fail now. Try as she might, this creature would not add me to her morbid collection. I fought against the grip with the surface mere inches away—but I found myself at a full stop just shy of my salvation. In a last-ditch effort,

I reached my hand toward the surface, feeling the cold wind brush against my fingertips.

As the world above drifted away, I felt a great force against my arm. With this, the grip against my leg mitigated into nothingness, and the surface came closer. As the ocean wind slammed into me, I had a feeling of unequalled relief. I gasped for air, this time unassisted. I found myself in tears between my elongated breaths. I was safe.

I opened my eyes to be met with the sight of my surviving companions, realizing that one of them had just pulled me from the depths of hell. Wordlessly, I rested against the floor of the lifeboat, unable to care about the destruction of my ship—my home. As I looked toward the beating sun, I realized that my survival was owed to the divines alone.

It was almost four days before we were rescued by a passing trade ship, though not all of the survivors were lucky enough to see their way back to the shore. I survived for some peculiar reason, though I doubted my worthiness.

Unsurprisingly, I decided to end my seafaring career after this ordeal. The sea, once my love, will now haunt me for the rest of my days. Nobody believed my tale, regarding it only as a madman's ramblings. I alone know what I saw on that fateful day, and I know I will never truly recover from the experience.

Sailors will forever speak in hushed tones of the evils that haunt the deep, but I know the truth is far darker. I know that what lies below is not the fabric of tales, but the solemn reality of the sea: While men may be the uncontested rulers of the Earth, we are nothing more than unwelcome guests to the strange and powerful forces that rule the deep.

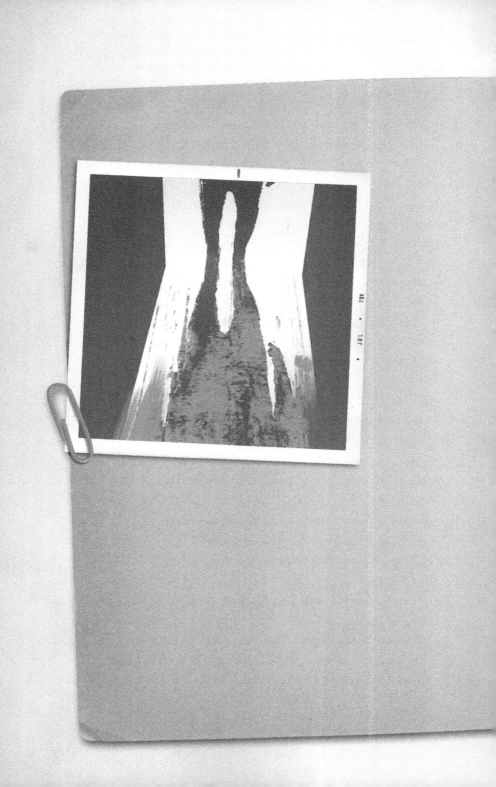

This journal was found by my grandfather, who spent a few of his early years searching the Washington shoreline for stories to help explain or corroborate events that had befallen his father.

After he found this, he stopped looking. To this day, the Vision is one of the most well-known tales of a ship's complete and utter disappearance.

THE LAST VOYAGE OF THE VISION

The horizon has spoken, and she is furious. She will no longer listen to our prayers, and all we can do is prepare for the merciless beating we are sure to endure.

The men are driven, but we've been away from port for too long. Supplies are dwindling and tensions are high, but I know that we are sturdier than the storms that await. This is just another of the sea's trials to test our worth.

Yet I feel unexplained anxiety. Through our countless travels, storms such as these have been common, but not worrisome. Yet something inside me churns with the waves. A paranoid foreboding has crept upon me, and it leaves me unsettled.

Some of the boys claim to see faces in the clouds. Some of them believe it is an omen of things to come. Many, like myself, don't believe these superstitions and delusions, but remain nervous. Tokens of faith and memories of familiar shores adorn our forms as we prepare, even if they're well-hidden to save our pride.

I have yet to tell them, but the winds are stronger

43

than anticipated. Without the stars, our navigator fears the worst. I can only pray whatever divines are watching will help us through this storm.

APRIL 19, 1890

That was no storm. It could not have been. It should not have been. It was as if the divines were locked in battle, and we were mere bystanders to their fury.

Waves broke over the bow almost as soon as we entered the gale, and we were nearly taken by the sea's hate. It took all we had to stay afloat—every ounce of strength. Cargo broke free and slid freely around the deck, causing mass chaos in the heart of the tempest.

I watched in vain as crates of precious supply took some of the inexperienced deckhands into the deep. Their screams were all but drowned out by the thunder, and the lightning was merciless. Twice I felt the shock flow through me, stopping my heart and slowing the scene to an agonizing halt.

I watched, unable to breathe, as our cannoneer—a man who knew the sea at its worst—calmly walked over the rails and into the murky torrent below. I screamed for him as he fell, garnering no response as his form disappeared into darkness.

My vision began to shake and my mind clouded with indiscernible thoughts. I staggered to the helm, looking down upon the men who fought so ferociously against the torrent. For a moment, I was able to focus upon the carnage. Hopelessly, I stared into the fray. Blood and water shimmered off the creaking deck as the bosun cried aloud, angrily screaming at the divines.

I didn't want to believe my eyes. More cargo slipped from the deck as the faces of my men grew pale, straining against fate, refusing to give up until there was nothing left.

Inspired, I began calling to my crew. Commands flew from my lips as I joined them, heaving lines and stowing everything that dared budge.

Soon enough, it was over. The storm broke and began to fade after what seemed like hours of torment. We had survived, albeit not without losses. Unsure of what to do, I stood immovable as the waves calmed. The darkened skies became bright eventually, and I was able to breathe again.

There was no celebration or joy, and none of the strained laughter that usually followed stressful situations like these. The remaining crew gathered what was left of our already-low supplies and their deceased friends, hastily praying over their broken forms before sending them into the deep. I helped move the injured to the sickbay before retiring to my cabin, collapsing into my rack and drifting into a long, unbothered slumber.

When I awoke, I was informed by the bosun that our navigator had not survived his injuries, and his companion had been reduced to a babbling wreck, going on and on about "eyes" in the deep.

We agreed to keep the grave news from the crew, and now, I write and pray that our hell has ended.

Though I know in my heart that it has only begun.

APRIL 30, 1898

The crew has surmised our damnable situation.

There is no escaping their hateful glares as I hurry about the ship. I fear for my life. Our stores of hardtack have run dry and the livestock we brought for this trip have begun to fade away.

Guilt pulses through me as I call my trusted staff to their best, each one doing the job of stronger men.

We can no longer trust the stars. They have lied to us and led us astray, further into merciless exile. The night that once guided us has become cold and godless, just like the crew I once called family, and I know I will find no brotherhood here. Crooked eyes and rusted blades glimmer in the dark, and I have accepted my fate.

It is no longer a matter of how, but when.

MAY 1, 1898

The ship's apothecary was murdered last night.

For days, rumors of witchcraft had followed his gaunt form, sending him into a deep paranoia. He refused the solace of my cabin, choosing to remain barricaded in his office opposite the sickbay.

A foul rot has overtaken some of the storm's injured survivors, scaling their flesh and cursing their skin with a pale, green hue. Their agony is apparent with each breath, and we all know they are doomed if we do not find assistance soon. Their only solace was the apothecary, and the paranoia of the crew has now ensured their suffering. His mangled corpse was desecrated when we found him in his once pristine, now gore-spattered office.

The remainder of my trusted staff assisted me in a hasty burial at sea in the dead of night, far from the eyes of the sulking crew. The bosun tried to make a joke, but the laughter was lost. The cook muttered a short prayer before we dropped our friend's corpse into the sea below.

As the realization of an approaching mutiny dawned upon me, I sighed.

It may have been my paranoia, but part of me believes that I saw a pair of glossy eyes follow my old companion as he sank into the deep.

As much as my heart begs me not to, I force myself to refrain from the paranoia in the name of my remaining crew.

If our current situation keeps, I believe we only have one week of food left, and maybe nine days of water.

I do not pray anymore. I know it to be of no use.

MAY 4, 1898

Land is on the horizon.

The coast of a distant island has mediated the tensions among my crew, and for the first time in almost a month of hell, I feel relief.

Yet as I scan the island for any signs of life, I am haunted by its desolation. The grey landscape is littered with twisted, unnatural vegetation and curious formations of salt and stone. It appears uninhabited, but from our vantage I can see small carvings in the stone.

The crew are awestruck. There is no fear in their eyes, only a long-forgotten hope. To them, it seems as if the divines were listening all along.

But the bosun and I agree that something is amiss.

As we prepare the rafts, I only wish I could join the others in their ignorant bliss.

MAY 8, 1898

That was no island. God, GOD—that was no island.

MAY 3, 1890

I still do not know what to write. I still do not know what I have seen; nor can I fully comprehend what I have survived.

The remaining men refuse to speak about it. Their pale, emotionless faces haunt me as we drift into timeless nothingness. Neither words nor thoughts exist in this endless suffering.

I was in charge of eighty men just over a month. Now, there are sixteen. So many brave men swallowed by both the fury of the sea and what lurks beneath it.

The island was not solid. It was unlike anything I have ever seen. It was not uninhabited. The screams of the scouting party still haunt my mind, just as the vision of them being devoured by the creatures that overtook them is burned into my skull, having removed any hope of solace. The creatures, a vile ooze of some eldritch sort, wasted no time in their ambush. Where ten brave men had once stood, ten bubbling piles of night-black horror remained. The creatures moved unnaturally, sliding across the surface of the water and onto my vessel, where they attacked my crew with a ferocity beyond my greatest nightmares. Sabers and rifles had no effect on their cursed forms—they simply ignored the blows as they overtook even the strongest of the crew.

The surviving men piled into a small cabin, and we stood in awe of the godless torment that awaited us. We huddled—some sobbing—trying to think of any possible escape.

After several minutes of listening to the creatures barraging the wooden door that held them from us, the cook had had enough. He ushered us through the cabins, instructing us to hide as he took another of our bravest souls to his side. He demanded that we stay quiet and wait for a signal, upon which we were to emerge from our ramshackle fortification. We agreed, though none of us believed salvation was possible.

After a few minutes of silence, a loud blast shook our cabin, followed by another. The hull jerked, as once again, against all odds, we found ourselves adrift.

Nobody dared move at first. Nobody even dared make a sound. Winds drifted across the decks and the walls began to creak and moan. The gentle swaying of the deck signaled that we were no longer close to any shore.

The bosun was the first to emerge from our holdout, and did so with haste. After a few halting minutes, he returned with a grim look on his once-confident face. He simply stated that it was "safe enough," at least for the moment.

We quickly discovered what had become of the brave souls who had ventured into the battle. Two smoking cannons told a tale that no words ever could. One, pointed at the anchor windlass, told the story of our escape. The other, set toward a still-burning hole in the deck, which was surrounded by specks of gore and gunpowder, told one of brotherhood.

They had prevented our demise, at least for the moment. But at what cost?

Now, the men wounded in the ambush have wounds similar to those injured in the storm, with the affected flesh already turning green and beginning to scale over, filling the air with a sickly scent of decay. The flesh of the men who were previously injured in the storm is almost completely overtaken by the scales. The stench is almost unbearable and we have decided to quarantine them until further notice. Their pained groans resound through the empty passageways.

I have failed. I do not know what is next, nor do I know if I truly care anymore. All I know is a suffering I cannot escape.

I don't feel like writing any more. I don't think I will any time soon. For now, the ship is mine to lead, and I intend to see us home.

?, 1890:

I am alone. My crew is beyond help, beyond human, and I am alone. I hear banging on the door as I write. God help me. If there is any left, I beg thee, end this torment. .

?, 1890:

I have escaped the ship, but to what end? Waves. Nothing but waves and solitude. I am alone on a lifeboat, drifting aimlessly. Days and nights have begun to blend together. No hope left. No honor. No brotherhood. No emotion. Only death.

August 20TH, 1890:

I am still recovering, both in body and in mind—though I believe the latter is a lost cause. I find myself now in an infirmary located in a town just off the coast of Massachusetts. Some time has passed, but everything is still so fresh in my mind. For the first time since the ambush, I feel motivated to write, to record, to attempt to find the words to describe what I have witnessed.

We had been aimlessly adrift after the ambush on the

island, for what had to have been months. The injured grew colder and more violent, and as their skin began to bubble and melt around the racks they lay upon, we knew. They began to chant and yell at the top of their decaying lungs—sounds that I can still hear clearly in my head. The horrifying noise drove the remaining men into the final states of madness, and all hope was lost.

We jettisoned their screaming forms into the abyss, but we weren't careful enough. The taint spread through the night as we slept. I awoke to screams from below, cries of terror and pain as a villainous laughter began to cross the decks of the ship. With haste, I crept from my bed and slowly moved into the passageways. As I moved, I observed the attackers from the shadows. They were oily, black, and emaciated, and smelled deeply of the same rot that had overtaken the injured few. They shambled along, their scaly skin reflecting the dim candlelight. They were hunting.

There had been eight of us before the night set in, and all I could do was hide while the cries of the remaining men slowly faded into laughter. The number dwindled until I alone remained, still sneaking toward the bridge, the only place I knew could be fortified enough to provide me protection, however temporary. Just before I reached the final stairwell that led to the bridge, I found myself surrounded on all sides by the mutated forms of the attackers. I was crouching behind a loose crate as they moved around me, sometimes mere inches from my face. Eventually, I saw an opening—a chance to ascend—and moved for it.

As I climbed, I heard a noise behind me that made my heart skip. It was one of the creatures, laughing as he neared me. I climbed the stairs as fast as I could, but the creature was close behind. I felt something grasp my ankle as I reached the top step, and fell against the wooden deck. Pain shot through my side as I kicked at my attacker, and I jerked my body away from it as I felt it release its grasp. I rose to my feet and began sprinting toward the bridge. I heard the attacker clear the stairs as I reached the door, opening it as he bounded across the deck. As I closed the door behind me, I caught a glimpse of the creature in the moonlight, a vision that will haunt me for the rest of my days. It was the bosun—or rather, had once been. His flesh bore the telltale signs of the infection, and his eyes were black and cold. A dark fluid dripped from his mouth as he neared me. He was still laughing as I slammed the door in his face.

When I close my eyes now, I still see that vision of him running at me, and still hear him taunting me as he pounded on my door, screaming for me to join him. For three days, I listened to them try and claw their way in as my water supply got lower and lower. On the morning of the third, they seemed to lose interest, moving further from the door and eventually belowdecks. In the night, I made my escape on the final remaining raft, with whatever supply I could scrounge from the bridge. The mangled, rotting creatures gave chase, but they were unable to follow me into the sea.

I know they remain there on that damned ship, waiting to strike. I pray that another storm takes it into the briny deep, far below the realm of the living. But I no longer rely on any divines for hope, for I no longer believe in any concept other than suffering.

I am between life and death, and the only thing my

mind begs me to do is decide—though I am too weak to commit to either.

I do not know how long I had been adrift before my raft finally reached the shore. Even more, I do not know how long it took for me to trust my surroundings enough to move inland. I eventually shambled my way into a nearby coastal town, where I was met with horrified eyes. I had not thought about what appearance my experience had left me with, but I realized it was nothing short of ghastly. I tried to tell my story, to convey the darkness that had befallen me, but my physical state and mental terror betrayed me. Eventually I was escorted to this infirmary, where I now reside. I recount the narrative to the only person who I know will listen: myself.

As of this morning, my sun-bleached raft has been taken by the authorities and I have no token to remember my once-proud life, save for this hellish diary. I no longer wish to write; at this point there is nothing more. No words exist to soothe the agony of my mind as I vainly attempt to assuage my guilt and endless dread.

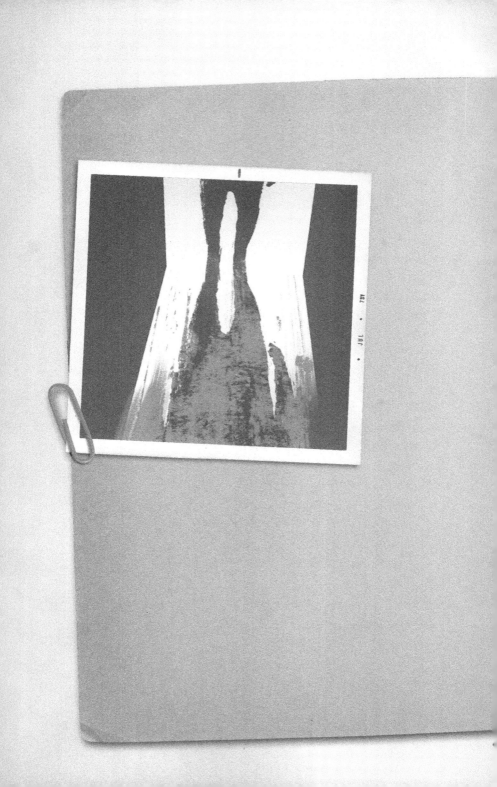

THIS DOCUMENT WAS FOUND IN A SMALL URBAN COMPOUND IN NORTHERN RAMSAY DURING A POLICE RAID. THE REPORTS DESCRIBE THE COMPOUND'S OCCUPANTS AS CULTISH AND VIOLENT, AND THE GROUP WAS KNOWN TO BE DANGEROUS FOR QUITE SOME TIME. THE AUTHORITIES HAD BEEN INVESTIGATING THEM FOR VARIOUS CRIMES AROUND THE AREA BEFORE A SHOOTOUT OCCURRED, EVENTUALLY CULMINATING IN THE GROUP'S MASS SUICIDE.

PAREIDOLIA

I'M TIRED OF RUNNING, both in body and mind.

Three days. It has only been three dark days since that horrible night. Three days since I last slept. Three days since my life ended and this hell began.

The chanting in the brush was too alluring to ignore. Many times I had explored the woods surrounding Ramsay, enough to become familiar with the common paths through them. It seemed to be a lonely, comforting solace. I had never seen another soul in these woods until that night, and I'm still unsure if I actually did then.

I was drawn from my path by a dim fire and furious chanting. I was far from town—undoubtedly, too far to witness anything civilized. My body told me to walk away, but my mind urged me on. Against my will, I obliged.

As I approached, I slowed, gently pushing the brush away from my eyes. I was at an overlook, and the fire was below me. I crouched and quietly crawled to the ledge, gazing toward the monosyllabic thrum that had piqued my interest.

I was greeted with a peculiar sight. Twelve pale men

in dark, flowing robes stood by the fireside, arms outstretched with their heads to the sky.

My heart sank into the pit of my stomach. My body was now urging me to run and hide, and this time I was going to oblige it. I began to carefully back away from the ledge, refusing to take my eyes from the occultists. As I gained some distance, I deciphered their chant: the words "Na-ma Ka Koreg," repeated endlessly.

As my view faded, I turned to flee. But when I cautiously began to step away, back toward the safety of civilization, a soft sobbing reverberated in the darkness. Once again, my body begged me to flee, but guilt and curiosity overpowered my senses. I turned once more, back toward the macabre ritual, and followed my silent path to the ledge.

I nearly screamed in terror when I returned to my perch. The men were still chanting, but this time, their hoods were removed and their faces were to the ground. The firelight did little to distinguish them, but that was of no concern.

What was of concern, however, was the naked woman, bound by the hands, who was now kneeling by the fire. She had seemed to appear out of thin air, and I silently wondered how I had missed her upon my first investigation. I identified her as the source of the sobbing, and I knew I could not leave her.

Alas, I was in no position to be brave. I was outnumbered, and I doubted the element of surprise would help me rescue her. She cried out, questioning the intent of the men, but was only met with their unbroken chant. She quickly became angry, threatening and screaming at her captors, demanding to be released. She continued, shouting expletives and thrashing until her voice became hoarse.

Still, the chant continued without any attention to the near-hysterical woman. After a few more unkind words, she began to sob again—this time seemingly resigned to whatever fate had in store.

I again tried to hypothesize a rescue plan, but still none seemed feasible. I became concerned with my own safety as I realized that they would only stay focused on her for so long. I grabbed a nearby stone in case I was discovered. I knew it would do little to fend them off, but if I had to, it would make for a momentary distraction.

When their chant ended, my heart skipped a beat. Sweat ran down my brow as I broke from my thoughtful trance. The leader of the pack raised his head, and I began to notice his features against the firelight. His face was heavily darkened by some kind of ink, and his eyes were bloodshot and glossy, glancing toward the hostage. When she rose to look at her assailant, she gasped in fear. She screamed for help and tried to move, but her restraints did not allow her.

The leader laughed heartily before turning his pale head toward each of his followers, silently observing their still-bowed forms.

He stretched tattooed hands to the night sky, and cried aloud in an indecipherable language, "Prth'na ju Nama'ka Koreg!" His body moved with his words.

"Nama'ka Koreg," His followers stoically replied in unison, joining hands around the fire.

They began to repeat the phrase—not quite a chant, but with growing vigor.

The woman grew desperate. Her movements were uncoordinated, limbs thrashing against restraints and contorting with obvious discomfort. She seemed to quickly lose control of her actions, jerking side to side violently, crying out in pain.

My jaw dropped. I gripped the stone tighter, now only thinking of my own escape. She was obviously doomed, but it had never fully occurred to me before this point. Tears welled in my eyes as I stepped back again, this time with no intent to return.

The fire roared with a newfound intensity, swirling in a semi-rhythmic vortex. The woman's movements grew more erratic, and her screams grew louder. The men's rhythmic voices once again overshadowed her pleas, this time assuming a seemingly accusatory tone. The woman screamed louder still, giving in to terror as she began to levitate, unassisted.

I grasped my chest. The pain in my heart was real, and the situation finally began to feel real. My breathing grew dense as the woman floated above the flame, no longer screaming in horror, but in agony—her voice fading into exhausted croaks.

The cultists began to chant louder, pleased with the evil sorcery that had overtaken the woman. Their chant turned to a cheer as her skin began to sear. Tears began to run down my face. My instincts told me to pray, to seek divine assistance, but I knew none was coming.

Now hovering mere inches above the fire, the woman's back began to spasm. Her screams turned to sobs as her torso began to fold before suddenly jerking into an impossible arch. All at once, the sounds she was making ceased. The chanting ceased shortly after, and silence filled the air. Time stood still as the flames licked the unmoving woman. My hand was over my mouth, stifling my erratic breaths. After a few painful moments, I resumed my retreat, once again not daring to take my eyes from the grizzly scene.

In my stupor, I lost my footing. I struggled to catch myself as my heart began pounding. I gasped, foolishly, as I grabbed onto a nearby branch in a failed effort to catch myself.

When I regained my balance, an uneasy calm over-took me. I slowly raised my eyes, only to be met with the vision of the cultists turning to me in unholy unison, their heads raised. I could no longer withhold my scream.

Aside from the leader, they were all missing faces. Smooth, lightly dimpled canvasses turned to me before freezing. I stared back, unsure of what to think. As hard as I tried, I could not process the sight. The cogs that powered my mind simply stopped moving, frozen in time and space.

They broke the standoff before I could. A formless, cascading laughter broke over the forest, seeming to surround me. My heart pounded as I realized that the laughter was not coming from around me, but from some-where within me.

I ran. I refused to become a victim to their macabre intentions, leaving them to their vices. The laughter did not slow, nor did it lose volume. It followed me along my escape, only leaving me upon my exit from the forest and my return to the familiar streets of inner Ramsay.

I did not break my sprint there, however. I breathlessly reached my home after navigating a labyrinth of back alleys and side roads. My lungs seemed ready to burst, but I was sure that I had put enough distance between me and the cultists to be safe if they chose to pursue me. I had not seen them since the forest, and their infernal, impossible laughter had left me long before I reached the door of my home.

I locked and bolted every door I could, and haphazardly barricaded any windows that were large enough to accommodate a human. For hours I paced, in an attempt to process the events I had witnessed. After I gave up, realizing that no sane man would believe my tale, I simply lay on my bed, resigned to a sleepless night. My mind began to wander as my body began to calm itself. I was exhausted, but sleep remained far from my grasp.

Upon the light of morning, I cautiously ventured from my dwelling. I resolved to seek divine assistance, knowing no other soul would pay heed to my encounter. I had been to see the priest at the chapel downtown a few times in the past, all in times of high stress. It seemed like a good place to clear my mind, and I knew the priest would listen to my woes.

It was only a short way into a long walk that I noticed that I was being followed at a distance. I could not make out any features in the bustle of the streets, with their usual mid-morning rush, but the way my heart filled with dread every time something even slightly abnormal crossed my peripheral vision was enough to keep me on edge.

Throughout the morning walk, the figure following me grew closer. It began with one person, then became several. They kept at a distance at first, but grew steadily closer with every passing minute. Upon my arrival to the chapel, I had found myself no less than shouting distance from them.

As I recounted my story to the priest, I saw the hope drain from his eyes. He stuttered as he spoke, simply offering me a blessing and a rosary before shooing me from his sight. At first I thought his reaction was due to his disbelief. But as I turned to exit the hallowed halls, I noticed a figure in the shadows, sitting in the pews furthest from me. One of my pursuers had entered. When he raised his faceless head to me, I knew.

Back on the streets, I knew that this nightmare had just begun. I wandered through the streets again, unsure of what to do. The forms did not cease in their pursuit. What once had been a far distance quickly became arms' reach. Twice, I turned, attempting to catch a glimpse of the men stalking me, only to be presented with the sight of the deformed husks growing closer each time.

Yet they never attempted to harm me. The closer they came, the more curious they seemed. They never spoke, never attempted anything drastic. They merely examined me as I made my way through the streets, filling me with discomfort. Stranger still, I was alone in my horror. I seemed to be the only one able to see these beings. My fellow pedestrians never once began to show the slightest sign of apprehension toward them.

As I returned to my home, I refused to barricade myself in. My mind no longer drove me. I had resigned to whatever horrors awaited me. If I was to die, I would not prolong my suffering.

Still, the beings refused to attack. They lingered outside my property, silhouettes pressed against windows, and shadows moving slowly in the faint light below the closed doors.

I awaited their intrusion, but it never came. As day turned to night, I had not eaten or slept, and I had hardly moved. Their restless shifting had found an eerie cadence, and I found them impossible to ignore. My mind raced with ideas as to what horrors could possibly come next. As the darkness grew, my sanity began to fade. I screamed aloud, begging them to explain why they had followed me. I pleaded for them to go away before I resigned to the floor, sobbing in a pathetic heap as their forms crowded my windows.

Yet they remained.

As I saw the sun rise through the dirty windows, their faceless forms remained. They had yet to act upon whatever they desired from me, only continuing their vigilance. In my panic-addled state I again begged them, this time to hurry and finish whatever they came to do, to release me from this torment.

Still, the torment grew. Their heads were now almost pressed to the glass, awaiting my next move.

I decided that I was no longer going to wait for them I fashioned my sheets into a rudimentary noose, supporting it upon a rafter in full view of the lot of them. As I climbed upon the chair, I stared at them—challenging them. Sinister whispers reverberated through the frame of my home, and I stepped closer to the edge of the chair.

Just as I had resigned myself to my sordid fate, I heard a soft creaking behind me. My instincts told me not to turn, but I ignored them. I turned, only to see the still-inked face of their leader. He stared at me, clear as day in the middle of the room, anger in his eyes. I sobbed again, attempting to turn away.

When I did, he was there. No matter where I turned, he was there. I screamed, not in terror, but resignation. In an attempt to escape his gaze, I turned toward the window. The beings just outside of the glass were no longer faceless, but carried the same face and grimace as their leader.

They all stared, all in anger. My body ached and my mind simply did not have the will to think anymore. I tried to finish what I had started, but the dread within me swelled as I moved closer to the ledge of the chair. I found that I could no longer carry on with my plan, completely lacking the willpower to commit to oblivion. I slipped my neck from the noose and curled on the floor, emotionless. The faces were no longer filled with malevolence, but were smiling. The same laughter that haunted me on that horrid night when this torment began filled my home. I closed my eyes, trying to shut them out, even momentarily.

When I opened my eyes, my tormentors were all above me. Almost a dozen of them, each still marked with the now-stoic face of their leader. A strange serenity washed over me as I resigned myself completely, unable to resist whatever may come.

The last thing I expected was for the one standing directly over me to stretch his hand toward me. A strange, emotionless invitation, but one I knew I couldn't refuse. My hand shook as I reached toward his, and as they met, something within me changed. A jolt shot through my veins, and with it, a strange sense of understanding. Alien memories flashed through my mind as the leader began to smile. Something within me had changed—something implacable.

My hand slipped away and I felt exhausted. Unable to move, I watched as day began to fade to night—with it, the faceless men began to fade as well. One by one, they began to back away—to leave my sight and disappear completely. The laughter and whispers soon stopped entirely, replaced by eerie silence.

I should feel relieved, but alas, I do not.

I know there is something bigger here. This occult sorcery has ruined me, but still, I grow curious. They had known what was to happen and calculated my every move. The visions were strange and completely unnatural, but felt inviting. They were trying to send a message, and I think I understand now.

It has been a few hours since their departure, and soon I shall move into the night—back to the forest, where this hell began. They have not spared me, but I now know that they never wished to harm me. I doubt that their will toward me was ill-natured in the least.

Something beyond my grasp has called me, by way of those infernal cultists. If that hadn't been the case, I would have perished long ago.

I am setting out into the unknown—an unknown that will welcome me with open arms. I do not know what is to follow, but I if I am correct, and these visions have shown me what I think they have, I will soon understand far more than I ever wished to know. The first vision was only a taste of that knowledge. Now that I've seen it, I must have more.

I see a lone faceless man in the distance, far beyond my window. This is the final sign. I know what I must do now, and for the first time since this ordeal began, I feel no fear.

Though the faceless man has no way of showing it, I believe he is smiling.

THIS DOCUMENT WAS IN THE ARCHIVES OF
ONE OF THE MORE RURAL TOWNS UPSTATE,
NEAR SEATTLE. THE CITIZENS OF SAID
TOWN ARE QUITE SUPERSTITIOUS, AND MANY
OF THEM BELIEVE THIS TALE IS COMPLETELY
TRUE RATHER THAN LOCAL FOLKLORE.

CLAUSTROPHOBIA

THE RASPY, GUTTURAL CACKLING rose from the trees as the sun's last rays fell from the sky. The ominous laughter got louder as the last of the villagers sank deep into their homes, hiding from the horror that awaited. I alone stood in my prison.

The soil beneath my feet began to cool, warning me of the dangers that would soon surround me. It wouldn't be much longer before the first of them came, just as my aged grandfather had once warned. I tried to warn the town, I honestly did. Perhaps if I had been more noble—more of the man my father had been—they would have believed me.

Instead, I stood in my iron tomb, in plain view of the town that had condemned me, unprotected from the sharp, red eyes that had begun sporadically dotting the trees closest to the village. Something in the trees cackled with a malevolent violence that shook me to my core.

My grandfather's prophecy did not adequately prepare me, though I believe nothing could have. Not for the wiry, slinking bodies that emerged from the wood. Pale skin stretched over warped bone, crawling from the trees with their evil laughter and unnatural, jutting movements.

Heads bent at bizarre angles. Viscera hanging from matted wounds. Claws scraping stone and earth. Rotted veins jutting against gray skin and pulsing with cursed blood. The beings were coming forth to claim their murderous bounty on all I knew.

Long ago, they were called "drownies." A story used to scare rebellious children based on tales passed down from the town's founders. The legend told that the nearby lake had been used by the long-dead natives in ritual sacrifices to an evil deity—and if the children misbehaved, the bodies of those who were drowned in the lake would take them in the night. This tale always scared me when I was a child. But that fear did not compare to what I felt at this moment, staring helplessly at the legend as it came to life, in a way more disturbing than I could have imagined.

They crawled through the square, toward the whimpering of the unsuspecting animals—left to die just as I had been.

The hounds went first. The drownies hunted them—hunted the whimpering, hunted the animalistic fear. Pained barks and yelps filled the night. An occasional splatter of gore made its way into my vision. I could hear some trying to fight, screaming as the claws tore them apart.

I wanted to cry, but I knew I couldn't risk the sound. I held my breath, feeling my heart pound against my chest. I had braced myself against the iron bars of the cage around me as the laughter began, and had refused to move since. My grandfather's words echoed in my ears as the beasts moved to the cattle, red eyes burning through the darkness.

He told me once, on his deathbed, of the drownies. He asserted that they were not a story, but something far more real than any of us knew. He told me that they came only on the coldest and darkest of nights to hunt all things living, acting on behalf of some eldritch power that none of us could truly understand. It was their curse and their vengeance. There was no stopping them; only preparing for whenever the time came.

My memory was still vivid, even after ten years. I still clearly heard my grandfather's breath, shallow and nearly inaudible, repeating a phrase that resounded in my mind endlessly as the cattle began to fall. "Be still, by god. Be still!" his dying voice croaked, over and over, just as it had on his deathbed so many years ago.

I had listened then, and I heeded now. I struggled to control my breath and my fear, as a light emerged from inside a barn on the edge of town. The horrors cackled on as the light grew stronger, overtaking the barn and burning into the night. It was no longer beasts that screamed, but men.

From my vantage, I could see one person panicking as the fire swept from the barn to his home, engulfing his refuge. I was not the only one who took notice of his desperation. The drownies started slowly crowding around the portal, simply watching their prey as he struggled against the smoke, faced with an impossible choice.

The man acted quicker than the monsters could. He raised his rifle to the window that sheltered him, took aim, and fired. The bullet struck the nearest monster, ripping a hole in its skull and spewing brain across the ground behind it. As he turned to fire at the next one, it rose again, cackling louder than before. He moved the rifle to fire again, but the monsters were quicker. One leaped with strength beyond any I had ever known, shattering the remains of the window and overtaking the man with ease. Two more joined, howling with laughter as he screamed. He fired his rifle again, but did nothing to slow the onslaught. The fire illuminated the scene, twisting my heart and forcing tears from my eyes. I was in agony as his screams began to fade, trying hard not to lose composure lest I join him in oblivion.

As the fire overtook his home, more screams began. A solemn realization overtook me. The man had not been alone.

More of the beasts crawled through the broken window, into the flames that had now overtaken the house. The screams got louder, bleeding into the night as the assault continued.

As the fire grew in ferocity, it spread, taking more shelters, and exposing their inhabitants to a death they could no longer escape.

There were so many. So many friends, so many families—so many innocent men and women. So many monsters, so many screams, so much blood. I heard rifles fire—some to fight, and some to surrender. I saw burning men leap from windows, screaming in pain, bringing the monsters to them to finish what the flames had started. I saw some try to run. None were fast enough. None were even close.

Yet I remained standing, anchored in this prison—this cage, my stronghold. My head pounded and my hands shook against the cold iron bars. My breathing was cold, deliberate, shallow, and coarse. The chill of the night tore at my skin and the worms from the dirt floor slithered across my feet, begging me to move, to escape this agony.

But I did not. I remained steadfast through the screams and the terror. My eyes darted around as I tried to find some escape from the carnage, but could not. Gnawed, broken limbs were scattered across my field of view—few of them attached to their owners. Blood soaked into the soil surrounding me, and joined the worms at my feet. I felt a silent scream, but would not let it out.

I merely stood, broken and motionless—an unwilling guest to the murder of everyone and everything I had ever known.

After hours of torment, the screams gave way to the cackling. The beasts patrolled the smoldering ruins, still chewing at the ruined corpses of my fellow townsfolk with their long, crooked fangs, cracking bone and tearing flesh as they carried on with their malignant display.

Tears no longer welled within me—all had been spent. My joints screamed in pain—begging for relief, begging for mercy, and begging me to move and meet the demise that I deserved.

But I could not. The smoke tickled my lungs as the sky grew … not brighter, but less dark. With this, I knew that the horror would end soon, one way or another.

The beasts had moved to the outskirts of the village, finishing their sweep as a few began their return to the woods.

I was unable to relax even slightly. I could not risk relief—not yet.

My eyes caught a slight, faint movement near the ruins of one of the nearby homes. Slowly, a child, no more than six, emerged from the grass—covered in soot, but alive. He looked to me, eyes welling with tears. His tears stained his face as he saw me and silently seemed to ask "why?"—a question we both knew I couldn't answer.

He silently mouthed something at me again, gently stepping toward me. I tried to shake my head—to warn him of the movement in my vision—but I couldn't. I screamed within myself, trying with all of my remaining might to warn him. But my body would not listen.

He took another step as one of the beasts crawled from behind my refuge, slinking around the cage and exposing its thin, pulsating body to me. I was looking toward the child, who froze in place, illuminated only by the smoldering remains of what had once been his home.

For a few moments, everything was still—a moment frozen in time, and a vision that still haunts my dreams, and claws at my soul with every waking moment.

Then the child whimpered. An involuntary, subtle movement, unavoidable in both his youth and his horror. The monster cackled for a moment, and then pounced on the child.

I couldn't look away. God, god—I couldn't do anything. I just sat, broken and motionless—helpless and useless in a hell that I could not escape.

The worms slithered between my toes as the cold wind bit at my face. But I was unfazed. I could barely feel it. My body grew quiet and my heart grew weaker. I felt nothing. Nothing at all.

Eventually, everything became quiet as the sun began to peek over the forest. The cackling had long faded, and now resided only in my mind. The fires had died down— only ruin remained. The stench of the dead replaced the stinging of the smoke, and the sun illuminated the true desperation of the scene I had endured.

Yet I still did not move. I couldn't—nor did I care to. I wanted mercy. I wanted the oblivion that I had selfishly escaped.

I do not know how long it was until the first of the survivors began to poke out of the ruins, from stone basements and small homes far from where the inferno had been.

As the cries and screams began again—this time for mourning—I did not move. As the broken men and women gathered—searching the homes for other survivors, and finding nothing—I was inert.

Even as the first of them pulled and twisted at the locks of my cage, I did nothing. I couldn't. I was comatose, but aware. Tears slid down the faces of the few who had escaped the torture—but mine were long gone.

I only regained my wits when a woman, furiously shaking in the morning chill, retrieved the key to my cage from the mangled corpse of a dead lawman. As she slid the key into the chamber, I shook violently, no longer able to control myself. I began screaming, crying, fighting her hands as she attempted to pull me from my cage.

A man joined her in dragging me from my prison, and my state worsened. I begged them to stop—to return me to the perceived safety of the iron bars, to take me away from the carnage. I tried to stand, but could not find the strength. I merely shouted, screamed, and cried, unable to process anything but the horror ingrained in my brain.

None of us who survived that long night ever returned to the ruins. No reclamation attempts were ever made or offered. We simply left—fleeing to anywhere that was not there.

I wandered for years—far from the carnage, and far from the terrors that had forever ruined my life. Though it is unlikely I will ever experience another long night with the drownies as long as I live, I can't bring myself to be anywhere near where it happened the first time.

I've found myself far from that curse—far from the doom that had ruined my chance at a peaceful, oblivious life. But in my heart I know I will never be far enough to escape the memories of that night.

THIS DOCUMENT BELONGED TO AN INPATIENT
AT A LOCAL ASYLUM, ONCE A STUDENT OF MINE.
SHE HAD FALLEN VICTIM TO AN UNEXPLAINABLE
MENTAL BREAKDOWN THAT, TO THIS DAY, HAS
LEFT HER AN INVALID. SHE ASKED FOR ME,
SPECIFICALLY, EARLY IN HER TREATMENT.
WHEN I ARRIVED, SHE GAVE ME THIS NOTE.
SHE HAS NOT SINCE RECOVERED NOR GAINED
ANY SEMBLANCE OF HER FORMER SELF.

NUTHISMIA: THE MISTS BEYOND THE VEIL

IN MY HAUNTED DREAMS, I see her forsaken eyes. They follow me, unblinking, through every restless nightmare and into the sleepless night.

Impossible memories resound deep within my mind as the horror overtakes me again and again, pushing me closer to the brink of unbecoming. Without solace, without mercy, I cannot escape her sight, just as I cannot escape myself.

The dreams began long ago, long before the harrowing events that cast me into this damnable fate. They began as implausible visions of the future, each one an infernal portent of the horrors to come. Every time I slumbered, I found myself gazing through another being's eyes, witness to terrors of both the familiar plane and far beyond. Somehow, I understood even the most inexplicable of the alien atrocities that I witnessed in my dreams, despite their existence far beyond my comprehension.

Over the years, the dreams slowly began to seep into my reality. Visions began dancing in my mind in my wakened state, and quickly became a common occurrence. As time went on, the intensity and frequency of the visions grew. I began to slip in between the realities, often confusing myself as to what was real and what was not.

As the visions became indiscernible, I began to seek assistance. Alien wisdom, tangible and implacable, crossed over from each plane, with my cursed self as the flux. With enough time and knowledge, I was able to quiet the visions while I was awake.

However, my dreams descended deeper into depravity. Whatever foul wisdom had been imparted to me had upset the malignant power that tormented me, and the power wanted vengeance.

It took all my strength to discern and cross the barriers once again, this time in search of the knowledge to find whatever power or being was causing my turmoil. My intention was to end the ordeal once and for all—something that both alarmed and delighted the beings I met in my surreal journeys.

It quickly became clear that while our realities were dissimilar, the dimensions that held our dreams were shared without discrimination. Hushed voices of towering monstrosities all spoke of the mists beyond the dreams, all fearing what lay beyond the veil.

I knew that there was something bigger drawing me toward the mists. I seemed feverish, hastily making preparations to embark upon my journey. Betwixt my feelings of wonder and anxiety lay the realization that I was to be venturing far beyond all I had ever known, or will ever know.

After crossing a few of the innumerable planes, I found myself at the base of a large pyramid, made from a stone that I hadn't seen in any of my quests. The stone vibrated softly and was warm to the touch. The gilded runes above the ornate doorway were in an eldritch language, one I

NUTHISMIA: THE MISTS BEYOND THE VEIL

had not encountered in my travels. I studied it for a short time before the runes gently slid together within my mind, mixing and shifting into a language that I understood. When the movement ended, the runes had formed the word "euphoria." With little hesitation, I pushed onward.

I was met by a blast of heat and an eyeful of colors, many of which I had never seen before. My body seemed to float as I was pulled to a tempest of color, sound, and light. My thoughts drained and were replaced by a torrent of bliss. For a few sweet moments, the waking horror that had plagued me was nothing. I was free of negativity, free of thought. I forgot pain and horror as I found myself swirling with countless beings of various dimensions in a pool of sweet, unadulterated joy. It was immaculate.

After a timeless bout in the vortex, my subconscious began to claw at the back of my mind. At first it was drowned by the ecstasy, but my uneasiness grew. Something urged me to look upon the beings beside me, and when I did, my euphoria faded into panic.

Their pallid, pale faces were seizing. Their bodies were riddled with tremors as their forms had begun to waste. Rapidly, I watched as the ones closest to the eye of the vortex began to disintegrate. The boundless joy had overtaken them, and they were mindless to their agony.

I struggled to break free of the vortex, turning from the visions. The vortex began to pull harder as the panic gained momentum. For a few moments, I felt as if the rift within me would tear me apart.

All at once, it was over. The vortex lost focus, breaking its hold over me, content with its blinded playthings. I found myself falling into darkness, the vortex rapidly fading from view. Gravity began to pull at me as I quickly gained momentum, eventually slowing to a light hover over an old, archaic hatch. The placard on the hatch read "Desire" in the same language as its predecessor. With no hesitation, I pressed onward though it.

I was met with the sight of looming, golden towers across a darkened skyline. Fine jewels caressed the horizon and augmented nearly everything in sight. It was beautiful in every way, from the air to the ground. Everything was trimmed, gilded with perfect adornments and fit perfectly together, as if the entire landscape had been meticulously planned and crafted down to the slightest detail. Gorgeous beings beyond my deepest imagination began to surround me—smiling, flirting, easing me into a lulled state that I could not shake, even if I had wanted to.

Again, my sanity pleaded with me to look beyond. The music faded just as the colors had, but this time, I submitted to the perfection of the scene, if only for a moment.

That was all the beings needed. Immediately, a grim, predatory glare fell across the lot. Gentle caresses became forceful grappling as the beings surrounded me. Their flawless forms began to fade into withered, demonic shadows, and the towers began to melt into a leaden blur.

I collected myself upon realizing the danger I was in. I forced the creatures away from me and began to back away from them. I paid them no attention as I ran, despite their grabbing hands and horrid screams. I would not give them the attention they craved.

Eventually, they gave up, just as the vortex had. New prey had emerged into the hunting grounds, and I had an unexplainable creeping sense that this prey was less resilient to false desires than I.

At the base of the largest of the melting towers in the

now-grey landscape, a single mirror sat. Above it, the word "terror" was hastily scrawled in the now-familiar eldritch language. This was the first time I hesitated. However, in my peripheral vision, I could see the foul creatures slowly encroaching. I continued through the mirror as the crowd grew. I prayed to whoever would listen that this journey was not a mistake.

This time, there was no bright light to greet me. Only darkness. I began walking, directionless. A distant, inhuman shriek pierced the night, alarming me. I froze, looking back from where I had come, only to see nothing. The portal I had entered from was gone, and beyond where it once had been stood a winged creature, hardly visible.

My heart ached as I realized what was happening. This time, my subconscious was nowhere to be found. A wave of hopelessness washed over me as the beast screamed again, this time descending to its forelegs. It began to sprint toward me, growing larger as it gained momentum.

I attempted to run, but there was nowhere to hide, no salvation in sight. I screamed—not in terror, but in anguish. The creature was more visible now. Eldritch runes dotted its macabre form, and a mass of tentacles moved across its face as it roared. Its fur was matted with the gore of countless beings, many of which I knew I had never encountered. Its mane was not hair, but stalks, each one holding a bloodshot, engorged eye.

It began to morph as it ran—each form more outlandish and demonic than the last. The runes burned into the darkness as my grip on sanity began to weaken. I laughed at the darkness of the situation. I had never asked for any of this. Yet here I was, about to be torn asunder because I desired peace with myself.

Suddenly, I found myself on the rotting ground. My body screamed at me, but my mind was silent. I turned just in time to see the monolithic horror stand over me, leathery wings outstretched beyond my vision. It looked down on me, roaring loud enough to shake my body to the core.

I smiled to myself. A strange serenity coursed through me as the creature's massive fists began to descend upon me. Unblinking, I watched.

The creature's fists stopped just shy of my face. I did not feel relief, nor surprise—only acceptance. After a few moments frozen like this, the creature began to shrink in both size and depravity. Eventually it gave up on me and fled into the darkness from which it had come.

Despite my confusion, I stood. I was beyond agitated with this journey. Once again, a small portal led to the next dream-cycle. This one was adorned with the word "Forgotten."

Before proceeding, I plucked a hair from my head. I wrapped it around my finger, predicting that this dimension would attempt to confuse and disorient me as the others had.

Before me lay every forgotten dream I ever had, as well as a complete collection of every memory within me, dating back to my childhood. They played before me, overloading my senses. All at once, the crescendo of senses crashed into me, weakening my gait. I thought I would lose my balance, but I somehow stood firm.

Quickly, my memories began to focus. They began forming into one thought and word. The memories began to split, and in the middle lay a single word—a name that justified my quest simply by the dread it brought me: *Nuthismia*.

Memories of my nightmares flocked to me, and began

to ascend into an unholy amalgamation of the horrors I had experienced, playing over and over again in immaculate detail. My head began to pound, and my hands shook. I looked down at my hand, only to see that the strand of hair it held had become a chain. The chain led to every forgotten memory, anchoring them to me.

As the memories began to overtake me, I untangled the chain. I took one last look at myself—one last look at the being that I had been when I had begun this awful quest.

With a deep breath, I dropped the chain, and the memories faded to silence again.

I took a moment to regain my composure. My mind ached, and my body felt wrong. But I knew that this journey was almost over. I focused again, and saw what had been teased by the guiding forces in my dreams—a final portal into the beyond. It had no placard, no label, but I knew what it was.

I climbed through the portal and was met with the essence of everything. This was beyond the veil—the crossroads of all that is, was, or will be. Everywhere I turned was another reality, another dimension. This was the delta of all existence, beyond the very concepts of reality and imagination.

I felt impossibly small and unimportant, but I knew that neither this crossroads nor this feeling alone was where the solution to my torment lay. I could feel a presence—something that guided me and challenged me to journey even further. After an impossible amount of time drifting through the formless void of the crossroads, I found her lair.

Beyond the edge of nonexistence, far beyond any

knowledge of anything tangible, I found her. In the mists beyond the veil, Nuthismia waited.

My drained mind had somehow held her name, but I never could have imagined her form. She was a nebula of raw essence, and she knew that this moment was approaching, far before the first thought had entered existence. In a mere moment, I knew. She was hidden here—perched beyond the existence of anything, divine or mortal—gazing into everything.

As her shapeless form contorted against the bleakness that surrounded her, I felt something powerful press against my very soul. In that moment, I knew she had led me here, and I realized that her dreams were not a curse, but a summons. Something within me began to change, and I felt a pain beyond any I had known. As I felt my mind unravel, breaking under her presence, I heard her whisper something to me. It was not a word, but an immaculate warning spoken by something that transcended language.

My mind flickered, and I lost myself in what I was becoming. As it all went dark, I felt an equilibrium of nothing and everything.

I awoke shortly after, back in my original reality. I did not feel anything. No senses guided me. I tried to scream or feel, but couldn't. I realized that I no longer had control of what I had been. I was nothing but a thought within a mortal vessel.

I exist now beyond the reach of humanity. When I

close what I can only describe as my eyes, I see visions from beyond the veil, from the eyes of Nuthismia herself. I see horrible things, godless things—and I know there is no escape.

For now, I've projected myself into control of this vessel—a being separate from the one that once was my own. I fear that upon my departure, when my essence will inevitably return to that space beyond the veil, sanity will leave with me. Her warning was not meant for me, but for them—the ones who exist in all that is tangible.

I have seen what lies ahead, in the twilight of eons that will come and pass as they please. I know that there is something that Nuthismia fears, and I know that I am not alone. I do not know why she has given me this curse, but I feel her eyes burning into me as I finish this testament.

The knowledge she has given me was never meant to save anyone. Rather, I believe I exist only as a witness to the end that is to come, whenever it may be.

I know that despite her divinity and knowledge, there are things far worse than either of us can begin to comprehend, waiting just beyond her sight for their chance to cross the veil.

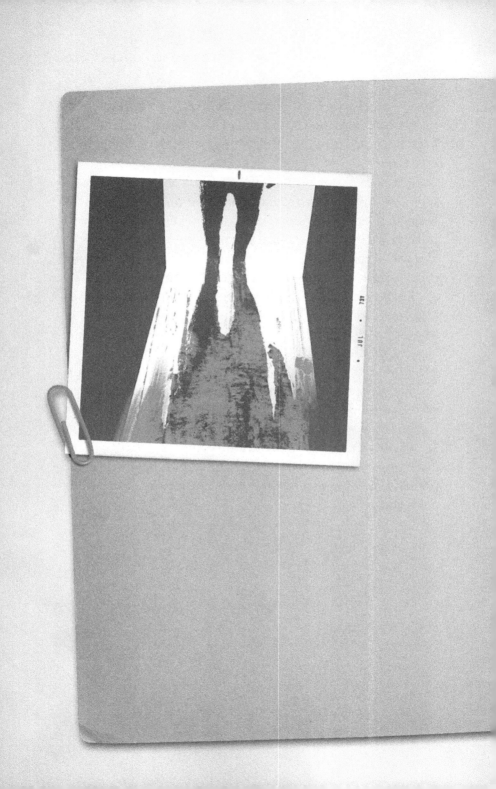

This document was found at the home of an extremist who committed various violent crimes across the Pacific Northwest. Sources state that he had been in and out of legal troubles for years. Many who knew him say that something had changed recently, and never suspected him capable of the terrible things he had done. He received the death penalty for his crime spree, but to the very end, remained unrepentant and indifferent toward the terror he caused.

THE MIDNIGHT OIL

UNDER THE SHROUD OF unrestrained euphoria, I met a drug-addled wanderer who spoke of the lies he'd been told and the fallacies he'd believed. He challenged all I had ever known in the brilliant darkness of the opiate-laden night.

As the wheels of the train we stowed ourselves in clicked along the rusted tracks, his voice followed, with rumors of vast abysses between thought and mind, in which untold masses of endless mystery welled far beyond the grasp of our gods or the mortal men who mocked them.

Intermittently spread through his hushed words was a gentle riddle, a suggestion of things to come—things yet to be observed by human eyes. Fear washed over his glossy eyes as he explained that our concepts of knowledge and wisdom were only the beginning.

He spoke of a reality beyond ours, which had evolved beyond the arbitrary concept of honesty. A realm where knowledge is free, without bias. All is known, and nothing is questioned. My curiosity was fed, and his words spoke through my intoxication. He warned of the horrors to be witnessed and the dangers that awaited me should I choose to journey into the vast abyss, but I foolishly chose to follow my wanderlust.

As our smoke rings filled the tepid air around us, my mind began to open. About a dozen flickering candles illuminated the unkempt cart, within which we were not entirely trapped, giving a dim light to various crates full of unsuspecting cargo. The rest of the train teetered along, oblivious to our reprehensible quest.

I was no occupational smuggler, but when you find yourself half a life deep into a serious drug habit, it's quite easy to find yourself in unsavory situations. The crates that surrounded us had been filled to the brim with opiates—the very substances that had led me here. When I agreed to the journey I was under the influence, and it did not sound nearly as dangerous as it felt now, especially as an amateur in illegal matters of this magnitude.

The wanderer, however, was a professional. While he was still mostly a stranger to me, his quiet words helped to keep my mind off of our frequent stops, and off of the anxiety that had begun to pollute it. The realm he spoke of inspired something primal within me—something I could not place. It was somewhere between fear and wonder, and far beyond the bliss of ignorance. I did not desire to see it—I *needed* to.

The train braked once more, but this time a strange tension filled the air. I was not alone in my concern. This was not routine. The wanderer's nerve lapsed for a moment as he hushed me. Our worries were confirmed—a cold sweat broke across my brow as heavy feet trotted above my head. Foreign voices spoke an unintelligible language with a gruff courtesy and a hint of interrogation.

Visions of the cruel prison that would become my new

home if we were discovered filled my mind as my intoxication began to fade rapidly. I looked toward the wanderer, who had since regained his composure. He began to snuff the candles, save for the one between us. His face seemed different in the glow—something more malicious than the bliss I had come to know. As the voices above grew sour, I began to shake.

His hand embraced my shoulder, and a tinge of desperation crossed his eyes. He knew that my inexperience and nerves were putting him at risk, and I began to doubt his intention. As his free hand reached into his coat pocket, my heart began to pound. When it emerged with an unfamiliar vial filled to the brim with a peculiar black substance, I was no less anxious. He carefully removed the cap and produced a pipette before motioning to me. I looked into his eyes as he nodded, and I quietly agreed. I could sense that he did not think I was ready, but knew of no other choice.

He gently pushed my head back and gestured for me to make sure my eyes stayed open. I followed his request and watched as he began to squeeze the drip, producing a small mass of a black liquid from the end. As the drops hit my eyes, the world began to spin around me. The crates around us began to blur until only my companion remained, suspended in an unfamiliar realm. His lips pursed in an unsure grin, as he mouthed the words "Be careful."

The last thing I recall before blacking out was his face, twisting in the glow, as he snuffed the final candle. Darkness overtook me, and my mind began to unravel.

When my senses gathered, I was far from anything I had ever known. A chrome-filled view of a vast industrial landscape tore across my vision and seeped into my mind. Metal cables and synthetic flesh melded around me. I was lost as to the meaning of it all.

Electricity pulsed through the mechanical veins at my feet, gently guiding my eyes toward the jagged center of the complex. All around, the half-technological, half-living thicket expanded far beyond the reach of my vision. With no escape visible, I found myself following the pulsations, only half voluntarily.

Drones flew overhead, oblivious to my intrusion. Their wings were long and vascular, but their bodies were cold and metallic. Their wings did not flap naturally, but rhythmically with sinister motion, as if a metronome guided both wings to act in an uncanny, unfamiliar unison. I tried to keep from their sight, but was unsure as to my success.

Fluorescent light from a smoggy sky gently illuminated my trail, and my path to the center of the plane remained unobstructed. As I pressed on, thoughts began to fill my head—but all were senseless. Burning symbols and quasi-familiar objects clashed in my skull. Multiple times I found myself unable to move, stopping to process the thoughts without hope of understanding.

The trail became narrower as the path became suffused with an oily runoff—a pollution which seeped up through the air and floated into the sky. I found myself unable to resist the urge to touch it. As my fingertips caressed the tainted, oily mass, my thoughts began to click with a frightening haste.

Sensory overload did not spare me from a sudden

burst of new knowledge. The arbitrary concepts of time and numeration became moot as a vast collection of information pulsed through my brain, opening me to flickering visions of the inner universe.

I felt a deep peace with myself rise alongside an implacable sorrow. As the beauty of everything began to register in my mind, I realized the insignificance of the life I had once known. No pipe dream or opiate bliss would ever be able to take me from the knowledge that I was nothing—a mere speck of emotion in an ocean of chaos.

Then, as quick as the knowledge came, it went. As the visions began to wither, I realized that my body had resumed my journey despite my preoccupation. I looked around, realizing I was atop the highest obelisk in the vast industrial sea.

Lightning struck at the subdivisions of the realm, illuminating an endless plane, unobstructed and ever-changing. I traced the bolts' paths across the acrid sky, eventually finding the horrifying center of the storm.

At the center lay a grotesque mass of flesh and machinery, bending and shifting its accursed form in the dim light of the broken sky. The mass was an eye, but not like any I had known. Within its oculus was displayed a cascading mass of symbols—some familiar, some alien. The cascade hinted at everything that ever was, even with a mere glance. All information, all truths, every cog of the inner universe moving in a perfect synthesis, held just beyond the form's iris. I am unsure of how I truly knew this, but the feeling I got was unmistakable. As I stared, no personal thoughts existed within me. No fear, no doubt—only existence.

A guiding feeling crossed my skin and moved my

form, fully opening me to the being. A crooked, half-living tendril sprouted from behind the eye, and began to jolt toward me. I did not desire to evade it. On the contrary, I waited patiently.

As the massive tendril closed in on me, I felt my humanity began to unravel. I had no sympathy or grief to feel by the time the tendril met the flesh between my eyes. In that moment, I became everything. The knowledge that had made me bend and wither once before had now been opened to me, and I felt myself slip between the confines of everything that is, was, could, or will be. As the tendril broke away, I was free of any mental confinement.

My enlightened mind shifted as the world around it began to slip away. My perception returned to my previous form, still aboard the train, now far from the terror it had once known. The wanderer, curious and observant, was hesitant upon my return. He did not know what had become of the preoccupied fool he had known, and he was right to question.

As his body moved, I read him. A cacophony of voices crossed my mind, and each one alerted me to his thoughts. His body language spoke louder than his breath, and I could surmise his thoughts. The hive of voices told me to reassure him, and a strange feeling spoke in a perfected tone through me. With a few simple words, I got him to believe me.

As our journey came to an end, he remained clueless as to my awakened form. I asked him if he had used the oil before. He had, but told me that he never had the courage to journey too deeply—only far enough to catch a taste of what was available. As he spoke, the voices informed me that on the contrary, he had never been strong enough to be welcomed as I had. I could sense his fear, but careful words and gestures assured him of my humanity while showing me the power that had awakened within me.

The sun gleamed over an eastern horizon as we agreed to part ways, his payment accurate and his words short.

The thoughts of intoxicating bliss no longer hold me within their clutches. The only bliss I know now is the gentle voices of the others who have taken my journey, who have made themselves known in the short time since my awakening. The hive of voices speaks to me and points me onward as their collective lull reaches a gentle harmony. My mind opens again, this time showing me visions from other beings, both wondrous and dark. Above them, the eye speaks, and it demands more.

The truth I found in the shadows of my mind guides me toward further enlightenment, and I know that I must share this gift of enlightenment. Eons and dimensions stretch before my mind, each one containing fellow enlightened beings—agents of the same abyss that has shown me this knowledge. Together we shall raise the eye from obscurity, back to the mortal planes of men, and praise the truth of knowledge.

As memories of the opiate bliss I had once known spill into my imagination, I know that they cannot compare to the feeling I get within my expanded consciousness as my voice joins the harmony, screaming in beautiful unison for the eye's return.

The eye is hungry, insatiable. It craves more—craves the vast absolution that it has offered me. Within the hive, the voices speak of the coming dawn—a time when no dangerous thought exists in the sea of knowledge. A time when the true name of the eye is restored and all mortals shall come to worship it.

I know on that day I shall stand again on the obelisk, under the truest form of the unblinking eye. The voices cry for him—for sacrifice, for unity, for the true name to be known again. I will do anything to bring that time nearer, and as I feel the primal strength surge within this vessel, I know that the voices are beginning to show me the way.

Soon the world will know the beauty of the hive, the knowledge of the eye, and the perfection that is Koreg.

This is the statement of Engels Lietrich, a renowned anthropologist employed by the university. He had suffered a breakdown upon returning from a study overseas, and quickly deteriorated. I have no idea how much of this is true and how much a result of mental duress. This took place a little over seven years ago, and it still hurts to read.

OLREA

FROM THE MOMENT MY feet moved from the boat to the silt, I was unimpressed. It was so drab, so unoriginal. I felt like I had stepped straight into every overbearing, pretentious documentary that this slice of corporeal wasteland had ever produced. It left a foul taste in my mouth, yet I knew there was a higher purpose to this journey than my criticism.

In life, the only thing that gave me true purpose was the unknown. Not just the dirty little secrets of the world, but the nooks and crannies within. Nothing is sacred to those with enough greed, and I was no better than Judas.

The Borrahu Tribe of South America happened to be one of the dirty little secrets. Their tribesmen had scarcely seen the larger world around them—yet somehow, they had survived on their own for longer than anyone seemed to know. The locals feared them in a way beyond anything I had witnessed. It was a spiritual fear, a primal fear.

While most rural tribes would hang sacrifices around their homes at night to appease their heathen gods, the ones neighboring the Borrahu did not. They did not believe that their gods had any power over the mortal

Borrahu. Instead, their sacrifices were meant to appease the Borrahu themselves, and earn a bounty of mercy from the misery they knew that tribe could exert—a prayer of forgiveness for a crime they never committed.

My first encounter with the Borrahu was unforgettable. I was with a small group of volunteers providing aid to one of the neighboring tribes, the Koreen, after a tropical monsoon ravaged their slice of jungle. I joined them not only to help with the relief, but to study the culture of the area.

On our third night in the village, some of the surviving hunters returned from a hunt with news that shook their tribe to the core: Upon incessant inquiry, they skittishly revealed that two of their companions had accidentally crossed the boundary leading to the Borrahu's lands.

This revelation was met with grief and terror. The elders refused to let the "tainted" young men re-enter the village for fear of retaliation. Their parents cried with rage and abandon, muttering prayers between chants. Upon my questioning of their frantic state, they simply repeated that there was nothing they could do to assist their loved ones. The errant hunters seemed to have accepted their fate, though they swore their transgression had gone unnoticed by their oppressors. The night quickly became sleepless for the tribe, and my curiosity was at an all-time high.

When the morning arrived, the Borrahu did as well. Even the most powerful men and women of the Koreen fled to the safety of their homes, choosing to watch the developments from afar rather than face the coming terror. The elders led my crew to their dwelling, chanting loudly in an incomprehensible language all the while.

Only three of the Borrahu had arrived, causing me to question the Koreen's fear. The three men were large, sure, but the victims' tribe had larger. If they wanted to save their own, I had no doubt they could overpower the invaders.

At the same time, something was amiss. The three men had an oppressive aura, and merely observing them made me uneasy. They were almost completely covered in primal tattoos, most of which depicted macabre scenes of war, violence, and brutality, each interconnecting to become a mural that seemed to praise all that was dark and hateful. Their eyes were darker than any I had ever seen, and their warped and mutated features indicated serious inbreeding. They were ghoulish for sure, but far from the terror I had expected.

Then, faster than my mind could process, they acted. They encircled the wayward young hunters, who now cried loudly in fear. The hunters called for their parents, for the elders, but were ignored. One of the young men tried to move away, but the Borrahu acted faster. I only noticed the Borrahu's lack of weapons as the first tribesman struck. In a sordid display of teeth, nails, and brute force, the hunter quickly fell, torn asunder, a victim to a primitive rage I had never imagined. Another tribesman turned to join on the savagery but caught sight of the second hunter turning to flee. The third of the Borrahu reacted with impossible speed, throwing the second hunter to the ground as his malevolent companion joined him. Within moments, both hunters lay slain—broken corpses under the jungle canopy.

As horrid as the sight was, the grave spectacle had only begun.

I spare the details for my own sake. The Borrahu chanted while they rearranged the grisly scene into a makeshift ritual, seeming to mock the customs of the villagers who gave me lodging. They chanted one phrase—one burning statement, over and over again: "Ol-re-a!" They stopped only when their sacrifice had been completed. The elders were no longer silent, but crying aloud. My companions had turned away long before the horrifying ritual started—before the first bits of flesh and viscera were torn from the mangled corpses—and now I alone sat to document the display. As the tribesmen finished, they looked around to the shocked faces peeking out of the huts, as if to challenge their foes—a challenge that went unmet. They began to take their leave, but one stopped. He looked toward my dwelling and I found myself paralyzed. He stopped one of the other warriors and pointed, and after a short exchange they both stared at me. I was still too scared to move.

Then, as quickly as they had come, they were gone. The catastrophe then fully dawned on the village. Panic set in, and within moments, the peaceful village became an onslaught of screams and cries, interlaced with desperate chants and malicious argument. The denizens were doing their best to cope with what they had just witnessed while simultaneously preparing for what horrors might happen next, should the Borrahu return.

After a wild few hours, we were asked by the elders to depart. They told us there was no place in this disaster for us, and that they could not ask us to endure the suffering ahead. We did not disagree, and ruled our venture a failure.

I quickly returned to my homeland so I could document the experience, in part to attempt to find some solace or peace after what I had witnessed. I did not fully recollect myself until I returned to Ramsay, where I eventually found the words to publish my account of the sordid events.

As much as I wished otherwise, that was not the last time I would see the Borrahu.

My published findings were praised and celebrated as a look into the gritty reality of the uncivilized secrets of the unincorporated corners of the Earth. Almost immediately, it exploded into an all-out manhunt for information on the Borrahu, yet nothing but sensationalist garbage and groundless speculation arose. Nobody could locate the tribe, no matter how hard they poked or prodded. The Borrahu did not want to be found, and my heart told me that they would get their wish at any cost.

That was true, at least, until one team found the remainder of the Koreen tribe we had helped. They had been set upon in the middle of the night and slain while they slept, their bodies carved ceremoniously and displayed in a grisly fashion. With the carnage, one powerful, plain-English message was spread upon the walls with blood:

Bring us the scribe.

Overnight, I too became a sensation. Humanitarian activists and cultural preservation societies alike blacklisted me, blaming me for the massacre. The island's government took swift action—not blaming me for the horror, but blaming the "basic nature of feudal natives." This was good enough for most, who simply began to lose interest after the initial shock had faded. However, for some, this was only the beginning. Many "brave" souls flocked to the jungle to search for the Borrahu, and witness the savage nature of the hidden world for themselves. Eventually, after a handful of mangled corpses were found and around two dozen search parties were called off, officials cordoned off that area of the jungle, backing it with their ramshackle military. For a time, this worked.

I did not know how the Borrahu caught wind of my findings, but obviously I had upset them. The innocents' blood was on my hands in some way, regardless of who did or did not believe it, and I knew that this was only going to be the beginning if I did not give them their wish.

In the end, the thing that influenced my decision to return was the endless guilt that had plagued me since the news of the massacre. My drive to search the unknown and bring it to light, my quest for notoriety through discovery, my choice to bring the savage tale of the Borrahu to the world at large ... all of the destruction seemed to hold me in the center of the tempest for some unknown reason. I knew I had to see this through to the end. I knew that if I were to survive, I would be immortalized with my findings. If not, I could die knowing that I at least attempted to atone for my meddling.

So once again, I found myself on a somber trek through the jungle, being led by a spiteful yet handsomely paid guide toward the remnants of the ruined village. This journey seemed to take longer than it had before, possibly due to my overbearing anxiety and unbowed curiosity for what may have come.

As the ruins came into sight, my curiosity died. The pictures and reports did no justice to the hell that had befallen these men and women. I recognized most of the decaying faces, all grimly twisted.

The way the bodies were mangled would lead an uneducated eye to assume that a pack of wild animals had caused this carnage. That assumption was not far from the truth. I felt sick. I had seen hatred, and I had seen murder—but this was different. It was completely mad, but so vividly real.

It was not long before I realized my companion and I were not alone.

It was only one man this time. He was distinctly Borrahu, yet something was different. He seemed more intimidating, yet stood more or less the same as the ones I had previously encountered. He stared at me, unwavering, unblinking, yet without outward hostility. At the same time, my guide shook violently. He was not present for my previous excursion, but I surmised that his time in this jungle had shown him at least a glimpse of the macabre capabilities of the Borrahu.

We sat for a few moments, just staring, until the tribesman spoke.

"Scribe ..." He began, and my blood ran cold. His word, his single word, was plain English. No accent. No stutter. Just English. My mind raced, discerning the sheer impossibility of this situation.

My thoughts ceased as my guide fled. Within moments, the thick jungle swallowed him and he became invisible to the world I now found myself in, alone.

"Do not be as foolish as your companion," the tribesman said, our mutual gaze still unbroken.

As a guttural scream pierced the jungle, I knew. I wasn't surprised, yet shame pulsed through my blood. Another life lost because of my meddling.

With an inexplicable courage, I spoke. "What do you desire?"

"Your assistance," he replied, tilting his enlarged head.

My mind did not process this. It was the first thing that truly surprised me, the first thing I did not expect in the slightest.

"How can ... how can I possibly assist you?" I asked.

"Scribe, you think far too deep toward answers that are so simple," he replied stoically, yet with a mocking tone.

However, he was correct. I had over-analyzed his request.

"You want me to document something," I guessed, as my mind began to clear.

The jagged smile that shot across his face froze the blood in my veins. "Yes," he answered, trailing the last syllable in a low hiss, as his eyes shifted across my figure.

"Then by all means, show me," I began firmly, yet with forced volume. "I'm sure it's more pressing than anything we may accomplish here."

My sudden defiance was the product of what had to be my final surge of courage. I did not think myself capable of such a feat, and I was uncertain of how my outburst would be received.

The smirk slipped from his face, and my grasp of time slipped soon after that. I could not bring myself to look away from the tribesman as his gaze pierced me. Terror welled within me as my vision focused on him, and only on him.

He broke the silence with a violent laugh, and I began to tremble. Any courage I had once felt now slipped away, and I was at the mercy of his words.

"Fair thought, scribe," he answered with a sharp tone.

Time began once again, and my body loosened. The view of the trees—once beautiful, now tainted with the horror in my heart—seeped back into my vision.

"We did not think you would cooperate so easily," he said, turning toward the forest. "And we are rarely wrong in our assumptions."

The civility of the warrior betrayed my judgements. For a moment, I dared to think that he was not one of the savages who had torn and mutilated the youths of the village on that ruinous day, let alone one of those who desolated the rest of that peaceful village.

Yet his demeanor betrayed my hopes. Everything about him screamed dread and malice, and I had no doubt that this horrid being was only beginning to show me the carnage and malevolence that he was capable of, kindly speech or not.

"Come," he demanded, and I followed without resistance.

As we passed foliage of indeterminate origin, the forest grew unnaturally dark. The canopy above did little to dissuade the notion that the atmosphere was inhuman, or even supernatural.

Even as my feet met familiar soil along the borders of the lands I had once explored, I felt more lost than ever. As we crossed into Borrahu territory, all semblance of safety left my mind. I experienced the darkness of primal fear and the grimace of unknown danger.

I felt more alone now than ever before, despite the wordless guidance of the malicious ambassador who treaded before me. His steps were purposeful, as if he could see a path that I could not. Even as our trek descended deeper into darkness and uncertainty, his guidance was unwavering—impossibly correct among the claustrophobic, indistinct foliage.

My grasp of time was lost again, until it seemed to go by drastically faster. The sky began to darken rapidly, and what felt like a full sprint was nothing more than a shamble—as if we had passed into a separate plane of hastened existence in which my mind raced faster than my body could respond.

By the time we had reached our destination, night

had long since fallen. Yet, in what should have been pitch darkness, I saw before me a ghastly village in a clearing.

The village was built around a gargantuan bonfire that burned brighter than any light I had ever witnessed. The silhouettes of what must have been hundreds of villagers danced and chanted wildly around the blaze, screaming vicious songs with macabre overtones, covering the roar of the fire.

Their homes, nothing more than decrepit mud huts, were surrounded by a fence made of bones and viscera, both human and animal. It took a few moments for me to realize that this display was not meant for warning or safety, but for challenge.

My guide no longer attempted to lead me, but instead joined his compatriots in the ritual. He cast a glance back to me, revealing that his eyes no longer held an unsettling darkness, but now contained the absence of life itself.

Fear grew in my heart and gripped my throat with power, and I choked against the urge to flee. Atop the burning timbers, a tall, gaunt tribesman stood in the heat, leading the chant with grand gestures and loud shrieks that pierced the air.

As the ambassador reached his place, the noise and movement ceased. A surreal calm fell over the crowd as a man who must have been the leader, who stood atop the embers, spoke with a roar.

"My kinsmen, we have stowed ourselves in the dark, waiting for this day, waiting for this moment, as the outside world carried on without us!" He was met with a near-simultaneous frenzy from his subjects. He went on. "Lord Olrea long ago gave us all the gift of sight within madness, and thrust upon us the secrets of the night!" The crowd's frenzy gained momentum.

Spindles of thought raced within my mind. Though I felt guilt, I was somewhat honored to bear witness to their strange ritual. Their religious fanaticism explained their isolation and their penchant for violence, but I knew there was more. For the first time since the beginning of my journey, I found myself able to focus on the details of their speech.

The corrupted, gaunt bodies of the tribesmen swayed with the flames, and I found that their ambassador's grotesque form was not an exception, but rather one of the simplest mutations.

Flesh hung where it should not, and bones were flayed against stretched, warped skin. Many of the tribe reveled with growths jutting from their bodies, mocking what should have been extra limbs. Most of them were scarcely human. They seemed the product of inbreeding on a massive scale.

I should have been sick, horrified. But alas, I was intrigued.

"We have an outsider among us, children!" the leader yowled with familiar intensity, his voice tearing again through the night.

I expected all eyes to shift to me, all attention to turn toward my unfamiliar presence. Yet they carried on with their violent tribute, too deeply entranced with their ritual to pay any heed to me. However, as I listened, I realized that while the ritual was the culmination of something special and important to the tribe, the leader's words were not meant for them.

No, they had to have known everything already …

what was to come next, what their performance would bring. The words were meant for me and me alone.

"On this night, this wondrous night, Lord Olrea shall bear witness to a new beginning—a new era!" The leader's voice rang, and with every fiber of my being I realized that I had made a mistake in letting my guard down. A familiar terror grabbed me, but again I found myself unable to pull away.

The stalwart dance of the tribe no longer resembled a celebration, but a frenzy. The deformed beings huddled close and inched toward the fire.

"For tonight, my brothers and sisters, our celebration is just," he continued with a new, far more horrifying tone as the flames below exploded into a full-force inferno.

The leader was the first to be incinerated in the blast as the fire's strength grew exponentially. His form stood unwavering as his body began to unravel, quickly becoming nothing more than scattered ash in that fell wind. It was only a few moments before the rest of the tribe was engulfed by the intense flames; they continued chanting as they began to wither and fade into the same oblivion that their leader had met.

When their revelrous cries should have turned to a collective howl of unimaginable agony, they instead turned to a sinister whisper.

An uneasy quiet filled the air as I realized that the bonfire was no longer making any noise. The inferno still raged, but the excessive heat began to dissipate into an unnatural, gnawing cold.

Out of the senselessness that had befallen me, a mocking, corrupt, and hollow voice filled the air.

"For we are now one with the flame," the voice

continued, as the flame's colors changed to an unnatural blue and began to recede into a form I can only describe as otherworldly.

The winds of the jungle no longer coursed aimlessly across the canopy above, but were drawn to the dying flame. As the flame bellowed and groaned, a putrid stench filled the air.

Broken limbs and jagged bone jutted through the flame alongside four long, bony arms. Tusks and horns grew across gore-spattered, ashen flesh as a walking nightmare rose before me. It resembled the Borrahu—gaunt and humanlike, but entirely unnatural. My horror welled as I realized that the tribe had not been merely celebrating this foul monster, but actively creating it.

As the creature reached its full manifestation, stillness fell over me. I could neither breathe, nor think, nor feel. I could only be.

"And from the flame comes the judgement," a familiar voice chimed, continuing the leader's speech louder than before. My ears rang, but I knew that the voice was coming from within the confines of my mind.

A rush of clarity coursed through my veins as I regained control of my body. Yet it did nothing to guide me from this malice. I simply stared at the omnipresent monstrosity, silently begging for this feverish experience to end.

All at once, it simply met my gaze. For a few moments, I inwardly begged for guidance, but was met with the mocking laughter of the tribe.

The creature's lips pursed, and then it slowly began to grin. Before I could understand what I was seeing, it was over. I felt my mind falter momentarily, and darkness overtook me.

I do not know how long I was in my stupor, nor how long I sat fetal, unable to wrap my mind around what I had witnessed. All I know is that when I awoke, I was completely alone in the blackened ruins of that blighted village.

I wandered again, without human guidance—back into the jungle from whence I had come. I did not question how I knew where to go. In my heart, I sensed that I was not in control, but was instead being led by whatever entity had invaded my mind.

I have lost all comprehension of reality, for I know it matters not. I know that I am recounting this tale without the creature's consent, but without resistance. As I close my eyes, the scourge's smile meets me and I cannot take it any longer. The only way I can make the terror that presses against my sanity cease—even momentarily—is documenting this tale.

As my tale draws to a close, my life will follow. The pressure around my neck is nothing compared to the mocking pressure in my skull, and I know that no simple reasoning or earthly means will explain how I found myself in these dire circumstances.

Forgive me, please. I desired secrets, but I never wished that these secrets would desire me.

THIS ENTRY WAS FOUND DURING AN ANTHROPOLOGICAL STUDY BY THE UNIVERSITY, FOCUSING ON THE DEVELOPMENT AND CULTURE OF THE RURAL SOUTHEASTERN STATES. THE VILLAGE IT WAS FOUND IN WAS ON ITS FINAL LEGS, WRACKED BY TIME AND ENVIRONMENT. WHEN ASKED ABOUT THIS TALE, THE LOCALS REFUSED TO ANSWER.

THE SONG OF THE SWAMP

A TEPID BREEZE FLOWS through the winding canals of this acrid swamp, bringing with it a gentle tune that is nearly inaudible in the sheer vastness of the unknown.

To most, it is impossible to notice. But for an unlucky few, it is paralyzing. Through the dense vegetation, it drifts, bringing haunting memories to any who have dared venture too deep into the wretched bog that originated it.

Every time the tune invades my mind, the memories of my experience with its creator intensify, bringing me back to the moment that stole my will and forever blurred the lines of reality and madness.

For as long as anyone cares to remember, my ancestors have dwelled among the towns surrounding this accursed bog. They have resided in shacks and shantytowns like my own, each one connected to the surrounding bayous and following their layout from the outskirts of Baton Rouge to the Atlantic itself. They've travelled, they've searched, and they've experienced vast and beautiful things. But each has returned, never to leave again.

My father was what the local populace called a mirewalker. His time away from the bog had been short, and he insisted that something about the ruined swamp drew him back and refused to let him leave. Before I was born, he frequently ventured into the bog, taking any poor soul with enough money along for the "adventure," as he called it.

When he spoke of his adventures, I could always tell that he was hiding something behind his tired eyes and half-hearted smile. The stories always ended abruptly, and as I aged, I realized that most of the endings were fabricated. When I was an adolescent, finally brave enough to question this, he stopped telling me his tales. Not long after, I stopped asking.

As I grew old enough to properly care for myself in the later part of my teenage years, he began his adventures again. The locals hailed him as a hero, but never explained why. Many strangers foreign to our town knew his name, but spoke in hushed tones when referring to his employment. I always wanted to know more, but did not want to pester him with something he did not desire to explain.

Soon enough, the times without him became more frequent than the times we shared. His eyes, usually tired, gradually became more sinister and sorrowful. I worried about him, but every time I inquired, I was met with his usual dismissal and redirection.

Only a fool would have been blind to his uneasiness. His absences grew longer and more frequent, eventually leading to a month-long voyage that had me beside myself with worry. I began asking the prominent locals what could be keeping him this long, and each just stared at me with familiar half-hearted smiles and gentle words, all affirming that it would "be okay soon."

They were wrong. So dreadfully wrong.

I awoke in the dead of night to my door crashing open.

I tried to scream but a hand covered my mouth. My father stood above, silhouetted insidiously against the darkness. His eyes were mad and his words were jagged. He commanded me to rise and follow him, breathing heavily.

As I dressed, I observed him violently rummaging through drawers for something. My head pounded and my body shook as he found what he was looking for with a heavy grunt. He shoved it into his rucksack before commanding me, again, to follow. I complied—in fear and fear alone.

As we plodded through the bog, the sounds of the wilderness blared around me. I could still hear him muttering to himself, but this time it was not anger in his words, but a gentle choking back of unseen tears and honest desperation.

I was the first to hear it. The savory, swaying tune above the bog. It seemed to overtake the wilderness that surrounded us. My father looked back again, his eyes no longer wild, but pained. As tears streamed from his eyes, he turned away and continued silently. I wanted to speak, to scream, to run—but could only shiver.

We continued toward the song, as it grew louder still. The moon seemed to reflect the gentle notes, which replaced the familiar sounds until all else became faint. The song left me feeling entranced, and I had no familiarity with the environment around me by the time we stopped again—a fact that further disoriented me. My father looked back to me, but refused to look me in the eyes. He merely choked on inaudible words.

He guided me past a small, faded cloth that marked an exit from the mire, and the entrance to an overgrown grotto behind the foliage. His timid steps were slow and deliberate, each one full of dread. The alluring tune no longer gently reverberated, but overpowered my mind.

We eventually reached a small clearing, where my father stopped altogether. He no longer held back the tears and refused to answer my questions—or perhaps he couldn't hear them. As a mass rose from the silt ahead of us, a tremor began within me.

It was a silt-covered body in rags, ascending from the bog below. Its coarse hair was as black as the night, and its skin was gray. It seemed carefully preserved despite its heavy emaciation, and had a distinctly feminine form. Its twisted, jagged hands swayed with the wind as I realized that this being was the source of the song.

My father screamed something over the song, but I couldn't comprehend it. I turned to him but only saw madness in his eyes. The tune rose higher, adding a slight vibrato as the wind blew the hair from the being's face.

What I saw pushed me over the edge. Behind her tangled hair lay empty, clouded eyes and an inhuman jaw, hanging agape and displaying her mangled fangs, shining in the moonlight.

The song rose and fell with her jaw as my father screamed again—the only thing that tore me from the sight. There were tears in his eyes again, as he kept screaming, still impossible to hear over the overpowering noise of the song. By the time I could understand him, he was upon me.

With a look of pure agony on his face, he screamed again. His words were finally understandable as he brought his knife closer to my flesh. "I'm so sorry!" I stepped back, heart pounding with shock. He swung the knife toward me, slicing my arm and causing me to fall.

I howled in pain as he stood above. He raised the knife again, crying inconsolably.

In the stillness of the moment, I realized that the song was changing. As he began to lower the blade, the notes of the song reached an unbearably high pitch, bringing a pain beyond the wound on my arm. I covered my ears forcefully and cried out as my father fell to the floor. The shadow of the being grew closer as the tune got lower again, and I seized my chance. I rose, but was quickly interrupted by my father. He pulled me, but I kicked his hand away. His other hand caught the leg I was using to balance, and I fell again.

He used his might to subdue me as the song began to rise again—but I fought against him. He winced in pain as the tune pierced his ears, and I fought harder. The haunting tone of the song seemed to give me an unnatural strength as I fought him again, this time gaining the upper hand. I shoved him off me, and as he met the mud beside me he screamed in pain.

He pleaded as I rose again, turning his body to reveal his own knife protruding from his back. He begged me to stay, screaming in between familiar sobs. I refused to listen.

I sprinted through the muck, only looking back when the song ended. The monster stood above my father, who took a defensive posture. He screamed for mercy, but the being descended upon him. As her twisted, rotting nails met his flesh, she turned to me. Her eyes flicked downwards, revealing her bloodshot irises. With this, I turned and fled again, refusing to look back.

I tried to retrace my father's steps as his screams pierced the night. After a few moments, the sound died out and I found myself in familiar wilderness.

The sun had just begun to rise, illuminating my path well enough for me to make my way through the bog. As the familiar smoke above my town became visible, my heart finally began to calm. I began to cry, finally coming to terms with the events of the night. My arm burned, but I pressed on, out of fear for what I had left behind. As the edge of my village began to appear over the vegetation around me, I breathed a sigh of relief.

The peace was shattered by the familiar tune. It was impossible to pinpoint what distant direction it was coming from—but still, I heard it. My hands shook and I hurried, refusing to look back. It continued until two fishermen at the bog's edge noticed me. Shocked by my appearance, they quickly came to my aid, sprinting from the dock across the traversable swamp. As they met me, I collapsed into their arms. I lost all composure before blacking out, my last memory being a glance of the malevolent being that had taken my father silhouetted against the edge of the dead trees from where I had emerged, staring at me as I lost consciousness.

When I awoke, it was days later. I had been in the care of a local doctor, who had treated my festering arm with care. He asked what had happened, seeming genuinely concerned, and I recounted my tale.

He dismissed it as a result of the fever. When I rebuffed his dismissal and insisted that my tale was true, he dropped his facade. With a stern, villainous gaze he repeated his claim, and in a hushed voice, urged that I forget the matter. I wanted to fight his command, but knew it was useless.

As I recovered, the story spread around the village. Many of the locals who were close to us offered their condolences at my father's disappearance, and commended me for my bravery in my "search" for him. But behind their words I knew that there was more.

Their tones were rehearsed, and their words insincere. Before long, I realized that they knew something that I didn't—something terrible. I refused to stick around and find out what it was.

A few nights after my recovery, I fled. I took everything valuable from my home and left quietly, promising myself I would never return.

I made that promise seven years ago, and it is a promise I can no longer keep. I've done everything I can to escape the memory of the creature, but in my dreams, I hear her song. The notes rise and fall as they did on that fateful day, beckoning me.

The terror has given way to curiosity and an overwhelming desire to return. From travelers, I have heard of the misfortunes that have befallen my old home, and I feel an irrepressible guilt. Something deep within me knows that their suffering and my departure is far from coincidental, and I know it will not halt with time.

Similarly, I've become the victim of horrid dreams related to the incident—dreams that have only grown more vivid over the years. I find myself unable to sleep, save for rare instances where my slumber is uninterrupted by the haunts that I have come to know. They have taken an immeasurable toll on my well-being, and I know that they will be my ruin unless I return to that grotto.

For in my dreams, it is no longer her song alone that beckons me, but her twisted, gangly form. It no longer seems evil, but welcoming. In my dreams, her familiar brow furrows at the sight of me, showing me that she recognizes and has knowledge of something terrible that is impossible to repress any longer: the implacable sense of a maternal warmth.

With this, I depart. For I shall no longer gaze into her eyes in my dreams, but meet them with my own. I can no longer refuse the familial similarity between us, which has haunted me every day for these seven long years—just as I can no longer refuse the allure of meeting her again.

THIS ONE IS PERSONAL TO ME. IT WAS TOLD TO ME BY A CLOSE FRIEND—A FELLOW PROFESSOR AT MY UNIVERSITY. SHE WAS WELL-KNOWN IN THE STATES FOR THE STORY OF HOW SHE SURVIVED HER COUNTRY'S DICTATORSHIP, TOLD TO COUNTLESS CROWDS DURING POLITICAL SEMINARS. I COULD ALWAYS TELL SHE WAS HIDING SOMETHING FROM THE PUBLIC, HOWEVER. IT TOOK ME YEARS TO GET HER TO OPEN UP, AND THIS IS THE RESULT.

THE EMPEROR'S NEW CLOTHES

WHOEVER DARED IMPLY THAT peaceful protest was more damaging to oppression than any sort of violent conflict deserves a bullet in their thick skull—although I doubt that it will be as effective as they deserve. When systematic tyranny has been effective for generations, protest is paltry—and to the perpetrators, a joke.

My father instilled this belief in me from a young age. Through our years serving the emperor, the truth of it became coldly apparent. Neither the emperor's policies, nor his political platform were designed to accomplish anything beneficial for the working men and women who supported him atop their ailing, malformed backs.

As much as I hate him for what he did, I cannot deny that it was all he had ever known. His ancestors, from a long and "glorious" line, had exerted their power alongside their malice whenever an opportunity arose to punish their subjects—regardless of how small the transgression was.

Even from an early age, I can recall hearing snippets from my father's hushed conversations: mass killings, public executions, and villages turned to cinders. As the corpse-piles beyond the graying horizon began to mount, the foreign sanctions followed.

My father did his best to shelter me from the life he had known as a member of the emperor's inner circle of advisors. As I aged, the proverbial wall separating our worlds began to crack, and the darkness that he withheld seeped into my reality. As ambassadorial peacemakers from the more civilized corners of the world abandoned us, the fragile air of social progress left with them. It did not take much longer for the fingertips of fate to lose their grasp on the uneasy control that the emperor held over the land.

I was still somewhat young—no more than fifteen—when the news broke of the ramshackle rebellion in the south. Farmers turned to soldiers overnight, mounting an offense in response to the execution of a well-liked community leader. When they were routed, another rebellion sprung up in the north. The emperor, in his typical fashion, was vicious and preemptory. Examples were made. Families were humiliated, broken, and brutalized, only to vanish silently into the grotesque history of his rule.

This time the spirit of the rebellion had been too great, and the submissive nature of the population gave way to something fierce and powerful. Satellite rebellions followed, and quickly surrounded the capitol. When the emperor's council first heard the grim news of makeshift soldiers on the horizon, they laughed, believing that their warriors would solve the problem.

Few remained laughing as news broke of the warriors who had switched sides, joining the rebellion. As the emperor ordered all who had sought refuge in his palace to ready for a hasty escape, none remained laughing. He announced to his closest advisors—my father among them—that he had worked out a plan of escape, and ordered us to prepare to leave immediately. I had only seen modern automobiles in books before they suddenly filled the garden of the emperor's castle, where they were hastily packed with heirlooms and historic pieces of the failing dynasty. The irony of preserving the very history that had led to this moment was not lost on me.

As we sped away from all we had ever known, a hint of unease crossed my father's eyes. This was the first time I had ever seen this happen, and it incited a panic in me that simply would not settle. He covered my eyes as the few who had remained behind were cut down by the advancing army as they tried to flee, and he stroked my hair as I began to cry. When the last view of the city faded from the horizon, he uncovered my eyes and told me everything would be alright. I put on a brave face for his sake, but by the time we reached our hideaway—a large villa hidden within the trees in the scarcely-populated western countryside of our nation—I was inwardly inconsolable.

My father's teachings kept up the facade of solidarity, despite my inner turmoil. As the great halls of the hidden mansion filled with political refugees, an eerie draft of calmness and normalcy fell over the crowd. The emperor assured us that we were safe, and spoke about a final evacuation to an allied nation that would take place "in due time."

For a precious while, all was well. It wasn't ideal, but it was preferable to the rumored brutality that awaited us at our homes. After a short time, the emperor began to withdraw from the social circles that graced the halls of this hidden palace. Most took it as depression for his failure. Some speculated that he had secretly taken a new consort. Whatever the case, I had no concern. At that time, I cared only for the well-being of my father.

He had aged rapidly. My mother had passed long before the revolution, and ever since, he had become so entwined in the fate of his country that he was oblivious to the frailty that began to eat at him. After the uprising, that frailty grew. In his mind, he had failed—not only as a countryman, but as a father. Taking care of him never bothered me. I wanted only to see him happy again. But I doubted his depression would end.

When the emperor broke his exile and gathered us in the palace's atrium, a dim flame of hope rose within me. As his words of a coming time of change and salvation rung within the grand walls, that flame began to roar. I believed that the end of suffering was near, and the return to normalcy was nigh.

My father's state worsened upon hearing the news. He no longer attempted to hide his withering mental state. When I questioned his frequent episodes of sobbing and isolation, he merely turned his morose eyes to me, pleading silently, before turning away.

My paranoia welled and my anxiety was nearly impossible to hide. I questioned my peers, who were as clueless as I. The adults were nearly as lost. A few speculated that our deliverance would be an experience of luxury and divinity. When I found the courage to query an elder, a compatriot of my father, he smiled and gently pulled me from the crowd. He hunched his shoulders slightly to meet my eyes before calmly reassuring me, telling me that the emperor was going to make sure all would be well again. For a moment, he looked as if he would say more, but eventually decided to keep silent. He asked me to keep watch over my father as I had been doing, before returning to his business.

For a while, this was enough to calm me. Days passed, and an eerie shade of mystery overtook the halls. Despite the promise of change and salvation, it seemed like no preparations were being made. The nobles close to the emperor began to slowly separate from their social circles, banding together under close supervision of his majesty.

When all began to seem lost again, they called us together. My father, for the first time since our captivity began, emerged from his quarters with me in tow. His old, wrinkled face was stricken with an implacable pain, and he kept looking at me with his soft, sad eyes. Nervous, we assembled in the grand hall as we had so many times before.

The light was dim and the atmosphere brooding. The emperor's advisors stood near him, flanking him as he stood on a platform raised above the crowd. As the doors behind us closed, he motioned for silence. We obliged immediately.

He began speaking, thanking us for our patience and commitment. He spoke of a promised escape coming shortly—but his words were foreign to me. The sinister atmosphere around me took all meaning from his words as a now-familiar hesitation entered my veins. I was unexplainably scared. My father was cold. His face, steely and serious, was immovable against the words that sang above us.

As the emperor's words gained momentum, cheers sprang from the crowd. Tears were shed as the energy in the room turned from admiration to worship. However, I did not join in the revelry. Instead, I backed toward the door behind us. I slipped through the crowd with ease, reaching the door in only a few moments.

I fiddled with the door before realizing, to my horror,

that it had been locked from the outside. My heart pounded as the emperor's words took a deeper tone. I turned to the door again, now desperately trying to unlock it without alerting any of the crowd.

I nearly screamed as a hand seized my shoulder, pulling me from the door. Gasps rose across the crowd as the emperor's voice continued to deepen. The crowd no longer cheered, but grumbled uneasily. I was forcefully rotated by the force behind me and was met with the face of my father. Tears rolled from his eyes as my mind began to register the scene beyond him.

The emperor, a lively presence on the stage, seemed to emanate a strange glow from his skin. He began to speak of the room's inhabitants, uttering nonsense about "the greater good" and "being remembered in the grand revival" as he swayed violently from side to side. As the uneasiness turned to fear, the guards that flanked him began to join in his odd motions.

I tried to turn away, but my father's hand dug into my shoulder. I winced, but went numb as the emperor's words fell into a violent cackle. I tried to back away, but was unable to control my movements as the scene became chaotic.

The emperor's face twisted and grayed rapidly, garnering screams from the crowd. The crowd simultaneously backed away from the stage as the emperor's face stretched, tearing the flesh from his jaw and revealing a fanged maw with blackened gums. The garments around his shoulders stretched and tore against the protruding muscle, further terrorizing the crowd. They began to shift violently toward me as the bones in his hands cracked and shifted, revealing twisted claws atop lanky fingers. As the crowd finally came to their collective senses and rushed toward the door that held us, his guards joined in his transformation.

I turned to my father, horrified, and screamed as his face began to twist, too. "I'm … sorry," he gasped as his eyes rolled into his head, slightly weakening his grasp upon me as his transformation began to take him.

I tried to break away fully, but could not. I thrashed against him, only breaking free when the crowd careened into me. Suddenly, I found myself tossed about in a sea of chaos, no more than a mere ragdoll to the men and women I had known for my entire life. They screamed and cried, pushing each other in an attempt to reach the door—oblivious to the hopelessness that awaited. Breath escaped my lungs with every accidental bludgeon, and I found myself unable to escape the carnage.

As my vision began to fade, I felt a sudden relief. I regained my senses, and realized that my relief was only momentary. My vision centered upon one of the newly-transformed beings as it sank its teeth into the neck of one of the lesser nobles I had known for as long as I can remember. They struggled for a moment before the being grabbed his victim's shoulders and began to violently thrash against him. A wad of gore was torn from the noble's form as he fell lifelessly, spraying blood across the now-demonic form of the being that was once his compatriot.

I turned my head only to realize that I was now at the center of the slaughter. The crowd that once crushed me had dispersed due to similar assaults, and I found myself among desolate corpses. I crawled away slowly, looking for any escape from the death that surrounded me.

A stained window across the floor caught my eye, giving me a tinge of hope. I crawled to a nearby pillar to catch my breath, and mentally prepared myself for a desperate plan. I knew it was my only chance, and I remained sure of my imminent demise.

As the screams and cries rang in my ears, I rose with a tremble. My heartbeat pounded in my ears, and I drew a few deep, shaken breaths. I looked around, seeing only depravity. When an opportunity arose, I breathed again, and began my sprint.

My feet splashed through blood as I ran, and I heard an inhuman cry as I gained momentum. I turned to see one of the demons springing at me, tossing the corpse of another lesser noble to the floor as it gave chase.

My adrenaline surged as the demon neared, swinging wildly. I felt its breath on my neck as another form joined it. All seemed lost until the creature's hiss was cut short and it fell to the floor with a colossal thud. It howled in pain as I turned again toward the window, gathering the last of my fleeting strength. I crossed my arms against my face in preparation for the impact.

I crashed through the window, shattering it with the force of my body, and began falling through the air. I expected to feel the floor immediately, but a gust of wind met me as I fell. I opened my eyes, only to be met with rapidly approaching foliage. As my body met the ground, pain shot through me. The breath left my lungs as I rolled, and then sprawled against silt and mud. My head spun. The pain centered on my shoulder, the area that had taken the brunt of my fall. I yelped miserably and attempted to bring my free hand to relieve it, but couldn't find the strength.

After a few desperate moments, I regained control of

my body. I turned my aching form to the sky, expecting to be surrounded by the demons I had narrowly escaped.

Instead, I was alone. Broken, pained, but alone. After a few more miserable moments, I found myself able to climb to my feet, but only with the assistance of a nearby sapling. I retched, and turned to the mansion one final time.

Similar windows to the one that had undoubtedly saved my life dotted the second floor, all revealing scenes of muted, flickering death. I wanted to cry, but did not have the strength.

As my eyes finally found the exact window that I had used to escape from the carnage, I was met with the sight of one of the demons. It stood against the fading dusk, staring wordlessly at me with its familiar, pained eyes. I stared back, meeting its gaze for a few moments.

As an air of understanding passed, the rising sun met its face. It began to shudder and morph back into something human, this time bearing no resemblance to anybody I had ever seen. After a few moments, it sighed, and then turned its back to me. I followed suit shortly after, and limped toward the forest that hid the estate.

As twilight turned to dawn, I found myself in the arms of the very rebels we had once fought so hard to escape. They listened to my story, but remained suspicious. I begged them to escape, but they did not listen. Their scouts took me to their camp as their warriors turned to the emperor's mansion. I begged them to be careful, but they did not listen.

That night, the warriors returned. They were pale and mentally exhausted, but otherwise unharmed. They affirmed my claims, but noted that by the time they had arrived, the mansion was deserted. My heart sank, but something within me expected no less.

The next few hours were long. I was a relic of a violent, hated regime, a reminder of a past that had caused agony to every individual lucky enough to still be alive. However, I was alone, terrified, and no more than a teenager. The soldiers returned me to the former capitol, where every symbol of the emperor's power had been removed with surgical precision. Here, I was turned over to the country's new "rulers"—a small council of revolutionaries that had banded together in the midst of the rebellion.

After great debate, they decided to spare me, if only for the symbolism. When I imparted my story to them, only the superstitious few listened, and I knew even fewer of them believed me.

I did not blame them for their suspicion, nor did I particularly care about it. I simply thanked them for their mercy and shambled off into the remnants of my home city, aimless.

The years that followed took their toll, but I survived. I changed myself, letting my former identity slip into the abyss of dark memories that housed the terrors I had witnessed.

As soon as I was able, I left the country for the world beyond. I could not stay somewhere with memories so painful and evil. So I wandered into the unknown again, hoping I would find something to make the pain cease.

Now, I am more than a memory. I have broken the bonds of the evil that held dominion over my mind and my memories, and have moved beyond my father's sins. I have shared my tale, albeit without the true horrors that it contained, with the new world I now call my home. I am incredibly thankful for this freedom and opportunity, and have used my experiences to advocate for those around the world who remain oppressed—an advocacy I cherish immensely.

However, while many now know how reprehensible the emperor's actions were, few know of the occult happenings behind his reign. I have told only a handful of my companions the truth of what I saw that fateful day, knowing that the public could never truly understand the full scope of the horror. While the history books assert that the emperor and his cabinet all died during the revolution, I know that they remain out there, continuing their depraved lives without justice.

The trail that leads to the emperor and my father runs cold after that accursed mansion, but I know in my heart that their demonic actions did not end there. The ritualistic transformation was undoubtedly just one in an incomprehensibly long series—one that I know must still be occurring. I know that they are out there, somewhere, waiting for their chance to emerge from the shadows, and pray on the weak, as they have before. I do not know how long their actions have stained the forgotten histories of this world, but I do know that they will continue as long as they possibly can.

After all these years, only one thing remains on my mind—plaguing my thoughts and worrying me more than any memory I still hold.

The emperor's actions may have been detestable, but he had numerous allies around the word, many of whom remain in power to this day.

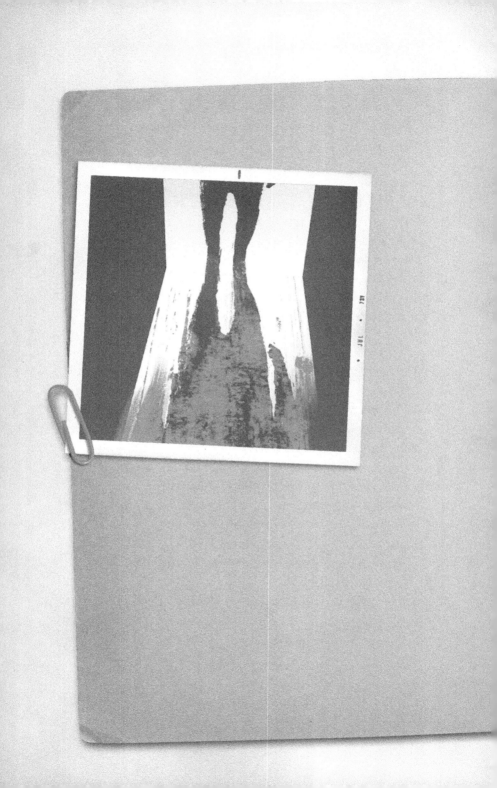

THIS ENTRY WAS FOUND AT A CRIME SCENE
ABOUT FIVE YEARS AGO. ITS WRITER WAS ALSO
A STUDENT OF MINE. HE WAS A TROUBLED MAN,
BUT I NEVER WOULD HAVE EXPECTED ANY OF
THE BELOW FROM HIM. NONE OF THE INDIVIDUALS
DOCUMENTED IN THIS ENTRY WERE EVER FOUND.

CABIN FEVER

I HAD LONG DREAMED of an idyllic life of riches without consequence, wherein every one of my desires were met with the haste that in my darkest hours I had long known to be my God-given right.

But such a life is only given to a few tactless, fortunate men, who do not know of the horrors men such as myself would inflict to reach similar wealth. For men with greed and desire like mine, the only option to sate the envy that had long since drowned the possibility of a life of normal peasantry was to work for it.

I had always known that my occupation would land me an eternity of suffering and damnation after my earthly pleasures were fulfilled. But never would I have imagined that hell would seep into my mortal life in the way it has.

I do not know precisely how long it has been since my life has taken this turn, but the memories of its beginning are still etched in my mind.

The job was supposed to have been easy. I'd been on many similar jobs, and as such, had dealt with the stress and misfortunes that had followed. This time, however, things had taken a turn into chaos and panic—a turn I never could have accounted for.

I still remember Terry's face as he realized he'd been shot. I remember his screams as Daniel and I piled him and our purloined riches in the back seat of our getaway vehicle. I remember the terrified faces of the gathering crowd, screaming as the shots rang above their bowed heads. I remember Daniel fumbling with the keys, screaming over Terry, pleading with a god he did not believe in for salvation through his bloodstained mask. I remember the engine firing as the officers emerged from their cover, weapons raised and ready. I remember the engine roaring to life as I turned one final time to the fray, firing wildly in an attempt to buy us a few precious seconds. Finally, I remember our vehicle speeding away as one of the officers fell to the ground, motionless.

That's where my memory turns to a haze of screams and anxiety. My heart pounded incessantly as we gained distance from the scene of our deplorable actions—my last remaining bit of adrenaline drowning out my comrades' screams as I struggled to grasp just how horribly amiss everything had gone.

I had never been a stranger to violence, but the memory of the officer falling to the ground—innocent, in his own way—remained vivid in my mind. As the paved roads turned to dirt and the mountains began to surround us, the memory remained. As we found our hidden refuge—a small, rustic cabin far from anything or anyone who would inconvenience our escape—it still remained. Even after the events that followed, after my life had turned further toward insanity and depravity, the broken face of the man as he fell stares back at me, condemning me to this hell that I now inhabit with my mortal body and mind.

The outskirts of the city quickly turned to the vivid colors of a late-spring tree line as our escape brought us to the surrounding wilderness, and I felt the air begin to thin as our vehicle began ascending the mountain road that led to our hideaway. It had been no more than an hour when we reached our destination, but felt like much longer with Terry's screams. My mind was scarcely present as we moved him to the house, even as his screams persisted. I led him to the couch as Daniel began searching for a medical kit that he swore had been stashed somewhere within our sanctum. Blood streaked the wooden floors, and began pooling under my friend's writhing form as Daniel returned, bandages in hand.

My focus turned from my guilt to my friend as we began our ill-informed procedure. Blood crept between my fingers as we guessed our way through our morbid routine, with only spasms and cries to guide us toward whatever remained of the bullet.

We did our best. When we were done, the bleeding slowed with Terry's breathing, and pained yelps replaced the agonizing screams. It wasn't pretty, nor was it what he deserved, but we knew it was the only option we had.

The night settled in quickly as we finished stowing our new riches and our car, giving a false but necessary sense of serenity to our momentary home. I had even managed to start the small, gas-powered furnace in the basement after Daniel was too scared to enter its dark depths—a fear that led to a fair amount of mockery.

Daniel, despite being shaky when it came to this kind of work, had ensured that the cabin was furnished and stocked well enough to hide us until we could continue our escape. But this had not accounted for the situation that we now faced. I reassured myself as much as I could, as the bitter cold of the mountain nipped at my face. But the anxiety would not leave me.

Terry tried his hardest to be positive through the pain, but that did nothing to soothe me. Even with the cold, sweat beaded on his brow. We gave him everything we could to help with the pain, hoping it would suffice for the time being.

I found myself unable to sleep, despite my exhaustion. The officer's face, Terry's screams, and the failures that had led us here haunted me. I lit a cigarette, laughing at the irony as I realized that I was using my "lucky" lighter—a memento of many previous jobs, which I always celebrated with a smoke.

As my mind wandered, my eyes followed. Through the window, I could see lights in the far distance. It was the glow from the city we had left behind—strong enough to notice but not enough to make us fear being discovered. A sudden, faint flicker of hope passed through my mind, slightly reassuring me through the silent cold. For a moment, I found a peace that eventually guided me through my unease to a deep slumber.

When I awoke, the peace fled immediately. What had once been the glow of the city had now become the glow of sunlight against a fresh layer of snow. In earlier years, I would have found this wondrous and mirthful, but I now found it horrifying. This had not been like any snowfall I had ever seen. The accumulation seemed impossible. This, like the rest of the sorrowful situation we found ourselves in, had not been predicted, nor prepared for.

I raced to the front door, still not completely believing that this turn of events was real, and passed a shallow-breathed Terry to find the situation worse than I thought. I pushed against the door with all of my might, but it hardly budged. I threw myself against it, again and again, quickly finding a panicked Daniel nearby. He joined me wordlessly, and eventually we worked our way outside.

Immediately, I felt the snow encircle my knees. I tried to bound over it—praying that somehow its depth was only an illusion. Mere steps from the door, I lost the few scraps of hope I had left. I cried aloud, screaming against the majesty of the mountains in pure, unbridled rage. More flakes fell against my face, insulting my stupidity.

I found myself unable to hold back, focusing my rage on Daniel, since he was the one who chose this cabin as our hideaway. Deep inside, I knew he was as innocent as any of us, and that this could not have been prepared for. But my rage blinded me. He stood at the doorway, oblivious to my intentions. My mind no longer controlled my body as my hands, cold and alien, grabbed at his shirt, throwing him to the ground. I brought my fists high, but he jolted away from the incoming blow with inches to spare. He tried to muscle himself free from my grasp, writhing and squirming as my hands brought another volley. I screamed obscenities and cursed him as I struck, blaming him for everything that had gone wrong—still without regard or control over my physical form. He tried to answer, but his words did not faze me. I grabbed him and held firm.

I know now that this kind of weather was highly irregular for the season, and this amount of snow was nothing short of a "miracle." But at that moment, that gruesome moment, no amount of divine reasoning or rational explanation would have been enough. The only thing that shook me from my anger was Terry's pained croaking—a successful attempt to grab my attention.

Momentarily, my mind returned. The only sound for some time was our collective breathing. Terry's breathing was labored, but steady. My breath, visible in the cold, was hoarse and aggravated, and so was Daniel's—albeit through a bloodied nose.

Suddenly, Daniel sputtered and grunted, sliding away from my hold. We moved to opposite sides of the room, and resumed our silence. I wanted to scream or cry, but nothing came out. We merely sat there, still, and tried to wrap our minds around anything that could bring us back to reality.

Daniel was the first to speak. He proposed that we venture out through the storm, back toward the town, and search for a doctor who was accustomed to our seedy line of work—someone we could bring back for Terry. He continued on for a few moments, adding that we could bring part of our haul with us to ensure cooperation, before Terry's voice rose above his.

He pleaded with us not to leave him alone, cold and defenseless. He was understandably terrified, but Daniel objected. He reasoned that there was not enough food for the three of us to wait this out, and began to speculate that Terry's state would further deteriorate. Terry responded with a pained whimper. Daniel then postulated that he, alone, venture out, leaving half the goods as collateral.

I objected. I did not trust him. In that moment, he was still the one I blamed for the situation at hand. Daniel and I had worked together for some time, surviving stressful situations, but this was different. This was far worse than anything either of us had experienced. It was obvious that our nerves were shot. He took offense to my objection, responding in a raised voice with obscenities and anger toward my character. Again, the anger overtook me momentarily, but I regained control after a few steps. Terry yelled aloud, ending our standoff.

It was then that I realized just how much he had deteriorated overnight. His eyes were glossed and full of tears, and his skin was far paler than it should have been. He pleaded, in short labored breaths, for us to stop fighting. Daniel asked him, mockingly, for his ideas. He, in turn, pointed in my direction. Daniel took even more offense at this suggestion. He refused, with a new slew of obscenities.

It took what seemed like hours of heated discussion for him to give way. During that time, Terry's state worsened. Daniel and I wordlessly searched the aged house, only finding a moth-eaten coat and a time-worn blanket to shelter me on my journey. We then watched the snow-laden windows, waiting for a break in the storm. After some time, I felt comfortable enough to begin my venture, pockets stuffed with capital, and embarked.

The oppressive cold beat against my face as I ventured on, plodding haphazardly through the snowdrifts as I moved further toward our only hope of salvation. With every darkening cloud, every increase in the snowfall, my confidence deteriorated into a primal fear that refused to leave my gut—but still I pressed on.

It must have been an hour before the wind picked up. All hope, rationality, and reason left me as fast as my vision did. The snow went from oppressive to overwhelming, and I began to lose sensation in my limbs.

Dread filled my very soul as I stopped in my tracks, desperate for anything real, begging any divinities that looked upon me for anything that would save me from freezing to death.

I turned in the direction of the tree line and fought my way to its cover. With every step, my form ached, and my terror grew. I moved between the trees, searching for a spot where the snow would not pelt me. But I only found myself moving deeper into the unfamiliar wild. My heart pounded, and I felt a chill run down to my bones as my body shook ferociously. I wanted to cry and scream, but only moved onward.

Just as the last ounce of sanity began to fade from my grief-stricken mind, I saw it. A small opening in the mountainside, almost hidden by the snowfall. With my remaining strength, I pushed toward it, through the blizzard. My only chance of survival. As I entered the cave, I could no longer hold back the tears. I could see again. I had escaped the blizzard's clutches, but the biting cold remained.

The cave opened substantially within a few steps. I tried my hardest to keep from slipping on the ice, but exhaustion refused me any solace. I fell, and struggled to rise again. This happened several times, but something deep within me kept fighting. Eventually, I found myself both accustomed to the dark and in a small clearing within the cave, in which the ruins of a humble campsite lay. I hesitated, calling out in a shaky, pleading tone for anyone to help me. I received no response.

I moved closer, spying a small fire pit with aged, dry wood that bore no signs of recent use. I moved toward it, passing a ramshackle tent before kneeling at my only chance of survival. I tried my lighter, but without tinder, it was useless. I cursed and fumbled under my breath before coming to a sordid realization.

My fingers could barely keep hold of the few dry dollars that remained in my pockets, and struggled even further to find an effective way of organizing them under the logs. Eventually, with persistence, the dollars began to catch fire, and the flame slowly grew in size. Within moments, the logs were completely alight, and I finally felt the warmth against my body. For the rest of my short days, I will never forget the feeling of the heat as I began stripping my soaked clothes off, exposing my blue-tinted skin in an attempt to get as much warmth as possible. That heat engulfed me—a comfort that I was sure I would never know again.

I fended off the desire to sleep, knowing it would likely mean death. The heat from the flames kissed my skin, making my body alert to the pain that still bit at my fingers and toes. I moved my still-soaked clothes closer to the fire in an attempt to dry them. My eyes wandered, searching for something to take my attention from the discomfort.

I saw a small stack of dry firewood, a few items that were piled haphazardly behind the makeshift tent, and a few other odds and ends that reignited a spark of confidence within me. My faint sense of safety lasted until I noticed a pair of well-worn boots and motionless legs peeking through the tent's opening.

I jumped, startled, before sheepishly calling out a greeting through my still-chattering teeth, awaiting a response that didn't come. I tried again, twice—both times pushing myself harder to raise the volume of my shaking voice, still with no response.

After a great deal of struggle, I forced myself to stand.

I shuffled hesitantly from the heat, toward whatever remained within the tent. Upon closer inspection, I found that the tent was in a much poorer condition than I had thought. The light from the fire shone through its torn canvas, illuminating the filth inside. I tried to peek at what I assumed to be its owner, but I could not see well enough.

I stood above the boots, trying to ascertain the smartest move. I called out once again, to no avail. My uneasiness peaked as I nudged the boots with my exposed foot, and felt nothing in response. I could hear nothing but my quickened heartbeat and the crackling of the fire as my hand reached toward the opening flap. Time stood still as I gently pulled it back, revealing its grey-skinned owner— face-down in what was no longer his earthen home.

I sighed heavily. I chuckled—I had never been so relieved to see a corpse. One less worry in a sea of mounting issues. I shook the boot with my hand—one final reassurance of the man's demise. With this final prod, I was completely reassured. I moved back to the fire, retrieving a small, half-burned log that would serve as a momentary torch. I raised the light to the tent, and struggled to hold back my screams.

The inside of the tent was torn, and frozen blood pooled on the rocks below the man, who I now saw had the appearance of a vagrant. His clothes were ripped, and viscera showed through. Whatever had taken his life had done so violently, as the filth from the poor man's brutalization extended along the cave's wall—a sight that I had missed in the darkness.

My mind struggled to adapt to the macabre sight, and primal instincts kicked in. I looked around, body still aching from my ill-fated journey. I knew that leaving now would result in certain death from the snow, but I knew that in my current state I could not withstand a fight with whatever had done this to the vagrant. I mumbled an empty prayer under my breath, and turned toward the darker, unexplored end of the cave.

My adrenaline took over, and I began moving deeper, listening for the sounds of my would-be demise. My heart dropped to my stomach as I moved, and I no longer felt anything but the numbness in my fingers and toes. A bead of sweat crossed my brow as my feet plodded against the stone, taking me back into darkness.

What I found was the furthest thing from what I expected. The path that led deeper into the cave stopped shortly beyond the fire pit, and it ended with a small stockpile of unopened cans, placed with care on a make-shift sled. I gasped, and laughed again, this time feeling a full relief. I was confused, but I struggle to remember a time I had been as elated. Whatever had taken this man's life had surely saved mine.

I moved the sled to the campsite, and added the remains of the torch to the fire. I tried to convince myself that whatever had attacked the vagrant had decided not to stay, and I hoped it would not return. I remained alert, but decided that if the danger was still present, I'd know soon enough. The cave had shown me no signs that it was currently inhabited, and I knew the storm would likely keep any intruders out.

For a few moments, I looked over the cans. They looked weathered, but had no true signs of degradation or rot. However, there was only one way to be sure. I struggled to open one of the cans, feeling the weight of my exhaustion as I resorted to blunt force. Eventually it split open, revealing a medley of still-edible vegetables. I placed the can and its contents near the fire and reveled in my fortune. In that moment, I felt safe again.

For a time, I forgot about the cabin, and about Terry and Daniel, and only felt the exhaustion. Using the last few ounces of my strength, I rekindled the fire and took a blanket from the ruined tent, and quickly found myself in a deep slumber.

I awoke with a jolt, expecting to be face to face with whatever horror had slaughtered the cave's previous owner. But I was met with only darkness and the low smoldering of the fire. My body again ached, but not nearly as bad as before. I could see the cave's entrance, basked in a dim light. I was still unsure as to the time. I quickly tended to the dying flames, using a few more of my remaining bills to ensure as little time in the cold as possible. My under-clothes had mostly dried, and provided me with small but precious comfort.

I noticed that my throat had become dry with thirst, and pondered for a moment before hatching a plan. I grabbed the remainder of the can, dented and torn but still capable of holding some contents, and began moving toward the entrance, seeing now that the storm was still blowing. I moved outside, feeling the cold grip at me again, but only remained exposed long enough to fill the can with fresh snow. I moved back, placing it by the fire, and waited for a few moments before drinking the snowmelt.

I felt mostly safe. I knew I could sustain this shelter for a small time—enough for me to recover and wait for the storm to die down fully before resuming my quest. I lit another cigarette before realizing that my fuel supply was limited. I groaned aloud, savoring the luxury as I decided to rummage through the remains of the tent for anything else useful.

I found a few odds and ends—a well-used piece of cookware; a mostly intact coat—before turning my attention to the vagrant's corpse. The threat of the cold far outweighed my respect for the dead. With great caution, I removed the remains of his coat, exposing the full brunt of his attacker's damage. I retched at the sight before resuming my macabre task—trying not to disturb the corpse as I began removing the blanket that he lay on.

I tugged on it, trying to wrench it from him, before quickly wishing that I hadn't. As the blanket gave way, so did the corpse. The action exposed his frostbitten face, still marked with a look of terror. His intestines hung from his abdomen, still frozen. I stepped back and tried my hardest not to vomit, gagging heavily. I fell to my knees, feeling them scrape against the stone below. I looked helplessly at the scene, unsure of how to react or proceed.

My eyes searched for something to pull myself from the scene, to reconnect myself to reality. I noticed a small, time-weathered book under the vagrant's legs—it had become exposed in the struggle. I moved toward it, grabbing it between my shaking fingers before pulling away. I shambled back to the fire, my refuge, and recovered for a few moments.

The book, a small journal, was perched in my fingers as the warmth once again overtook me. By the firelight, I opened the cover, exposing a hasty and near-indecipherable script. My eyes strained to understand, as I thumbed through the mess and eventually found cleaner, more recent entries.

I could hardly make out the context, or the reasons

that had led the man to write. For a time, all I could see was different scribblings about his adventures, detailing his travels and life on the road. The similarity of our stories became clearer as I read on, and a tinge of remorse slipped into my mind. He had survived with two companions—on their own against an unforgiving and hostile world. Like us, they stole for survival, albeit in a different way. My heart twisted as he recounted a tale in which one of his companions had been injured by a guard dog, leaving one of his arms almost completely crippled.

I thought of Terry, and of Daniel. My thoughts only intensified as I read on, learning that they had departed from the same city we had so recently fled—although their departure seemed less violent. I sighed, and felt tears in my eyes. I wanted this mess to be over. I wanted Terry and Daniel to be safe, and I wanted to be free from this nightmare.

As I continued, the story grew darker. The injured companion was beset by an infection as they ventured up the mountain. He progressively became more ill, and the writing in the pages got hastier. Eventually, they found themselves stuck in an old campground as the snow began to fall. Then the misfortunes truly began. The writer revealed that he had hidden a small store of food nearby a few months prior, in case of an emergency—likely the collection I had found. He further explained that as the snow worsened, the three found themselves confined to a tent, waiting with dwindling supplies—much like the situation I had left Daniel and Terry in.

My anxiety peaked as I read on. I could no longer hold the tears back as the story became far more gruesome than I thought possible. For the first time since my arrival, I felt truly trapped in this cave. The script further deteriorated as the vagrant detailed the death of the injured companion, and the looming hunger that hung over the survivors.

My heart began to pound as the pages detailed the other companion's slow descent into hunger-driven madness, eventually culminating in him acting upon his primal desires with the fallen man's flesh. Again, I thought of Terry and Daniel as paranoia overtook my thoughts. I agonized over my inability to act as the storm raged on.

With a morbid curiosity, I read on, knowing full well that there was no positive end to this story—nothing that would help soothe my guilt. The story fell further into depravity, describing the cannibalistic companion's deeper descent into madness, with the writer's mental state not far behind. Although he abstained from the flesh, he noted that the other survivor had been staring at him in a dark, unsettling way.

As the pages went on, they grew shorter, but the horror grew more rampant. The writer described how the other survivor's flesh began to grey, and noted that it seemed his teeth had begun transforming into something inhuman.

The diary further documented the other man's decay before abruptly turning to a clearer and more sorrowful tone. The author revealed that he had fled during the stormy night after the other man's decay had become physically and mentally unbearable. He documented a few days of sorrow in the refuge that we now shared, reflecting on his past and the loss of his friends before growing terrified and paranoid, swearing that he had seen something in the night that resembled his friend, but "was no longer."

What followed was an abrupt end. A small amount of pages remained, unblemished—a discovery that filled me with a similar paranoia and fear as the vagrant felt in his final days. For the first time since finding the cave, I realized how bad the situation at the cabin could become, and how much time I was wasting in my recovery while my friends' state got worse. I knew I had to act soon, for their sake. The storm had somewhat subsided, and in my current state I knew I would not survive another attempt to get to town if the weather got worse.

Inaction plagued me as day turned to night. This cycle continued for a few days, with me checking the storm for any sign of a break amidst a slew of fears that plagued every waking moment—fears for both me and my friends. My dreams were plagued with thoughts of the vagrant turned beast, still possibly out there, waiting for his next meal, finding the cabin, finding my cave. The idea ate at me, and I felt myself slip further into a spiral of paranoia.

I had lost track of the days by the time I awoke to a clear, unclouded sky. The sunlight reflected from the snow burned my eyes, yet filled me with enough strength to convince me to return to the cabin rather than try to find the doctor. In my stupor, I realized that my friends' situation was undoubtedly dire, but I needed to know that they were still alive. I gathered the few remaining cans of food, and the sled, which I thought would still be of use to Terry. I was afraid that they may have been found by authorities, or possibly escaped on their own, but decided that it was more important to know their situation than continue speculating and assuming. It was risky, but I couldn't convince myself that any other option was valid.

Before I gathered the courage to leave, I decided to double back and retrieve the vagrant's journal—if only out of a strange gratitude for my occupation of the sanctum that entombed him. It felt wrong leaving it—leaving the story to the same oblivion that had taken him.

I left the cave behind at what I assumed to have been mid-day, but found myself under a quickly-setting sun as the cabin first became visible. I do not know why my arrival was so behind schedule. Maybe I had misjudged my original trip's length; or my current, weakened state; or the added weight of the sled; or a combination of it all. It didn't matter. I arrived at the door and called out, awaiting a response as the sun completely fell from view.

I received nothing. My heart sank, and anxiety pulsed through my veins. I called out again, shouting this time—again, to no avail. I let go of my hold on the sled and pounded at the door, eventually forcing it open. Terry and Daniel were nowhere to be found. Instead, a bloody couch remained, seeming to amplify the silence around me. I cried aloud in resignation, unable to hold the emotions of my failure back.

It took a few moments for me to regain my composure. I moved quickly for the garage, praying that they had made some kind of daring escape during my stay in the cave. I found the car untouched, with its cracked windshield covered in ice. I moved toward the back, opening the trunk and praying that the money would not be present, which would have been a telltale sign of my companions' departure.

All hope fled as our riches stared back at me. Confusion and resignation again flooded my senses as I felt tears fall from my eyes.

Then came a noise—a gentle creaking of movement from just inside the house. My anxiety quickly morphed into fear as I searched the darkness for its source. I was met with a silhouette in the entrance of the garage and a familiar but pained voice.

"Where have you been?" Daniel croaked, unmoving.

My paranoia peaked. I struggled for words as it dawned on me that something was very amiss.

"I got stuck in the storm. I found a cave ..." I began, as he moved closer to me. He seemed taller—that terrified me.

I heard a faint crackling as he stepped forward, and my heart began to race.

"There was food. I got stuck, but there's a sled, and I—" was all I could say as he became visible to me.

It was not the Daniel I had known. It was something horrible, something macabre. Like the beast in the journal, his skin was grey, and his jaw malformed. His eyes were gaunt and his ribs poked though exposed, veiny flesh. His hair was mottled, and he shook as he walked. He stopped across from me, and simply stared at me with his sunken, bloodshot eyes. Sharp teeth jutted from his lips. I struggled to breathe. Sweat crossed my brow as I struggled to comprehend the ghastly sight, and a horrifying thought formed in my mind.

"Where is Terry?" I asked, sheepishly.

His form shifted gently, almost as if a breeze had crossed him. His bones seemed to shift below his skin as he stepped closer, causing me to me to back against the wall.

"Where's the money?" he asked, and then croaked again—this time with a hiss.

His breathing was sharp and hoarse, further terrifying me. We simply stood there for a few moments, staring at each other, suspended in a macabre moment of uncertainty.

I moved first. I turned toward the opposite side of the

car, and he responded with an inhuman shriek. I began to sprint as he climbed atop the vehicle, swiping at me with his malformed hands. I screamed as I passed through the door, slamming it behind me as I struggled to think. I heard him shriek again as he careened with the door behind me, tearing one of the hinges from the wall. I could hear him reel back and snatch at the doorknob as I weighed my options.

I spied the open door to the basement, where the furnace had been. As I heard the garage door loudly jar behind me, I sprinted for it, managing to cross through before I heard his footsteps behind me. I turned to close the door behind me, seeing him bound toward me like an animal on the hunt. I slammed it and struggled with the deadbolt as he collided with the door, with a force that almost sent me down the staircase. I pushed back with all of my remaining might, being met with another of his unearthly cries. I wrapped my fingers around the dead-bolt and moved it into its position as his hands pounded against the door.

I found myself at a small landing at the top of the stairs leading to the basement proper. I looked around for anything that could reinforce the door, finding only an old tool shelf. I struggled to push it against the door, which was still holding despite Daniel's onslaught. I struggled to catch my breath as Daniel's voice sounded again, with anger beyond any I had known.

"You can't hide forever!" he screamed, pounding the door a final time before grunting and moving away from it.

I listened for a few moments, trying to keep track of his position. The scene grew silent again, yet my heart still raced. I struggled to process the events that had just unfolded before descending into the darkness, searching for anything that could help my sorrowful position.

The only thing I found was Terry's mangled corpse. I stood over him for a long time, unsure of what to do. I hoped that he had expired before Daniel's desire had overtaken him, and thought of the vagrant's friend.

I then thought of the vagrant's fate, knowing full well that mine would likely be similar.

This thought has not left my mind since the beginning of my incarceration in this tomb. I've searched every nook of this basement, and haven't found the luxury of rest since I first barricaded myself in here. My options are limited, and I fear that none will lead to my survival. If I leave, Daniel will kill me. If he doesn't, I'll likely succumb to the elements. If I stay, I'll starve, or will be at the mercy of Daniel's desperation—for I know that my barricade will not hold forever.

This story has filled the last few pages of the vagrant's journal, and is only delaying the inevitable. As the final page draws to a close, I must conclude that I deserve this hell. I don't know if it's the hunger, the exhaustion, or the terror, but I see the faces of those I have wronged in the darkness. They stare at me, condemning me to the doom that awaits.

I know I'm going mad, and I cannot stop myself. As the stench of Terry's corpse grows stronger, and the sounds of Daniel's lurking grow more frequent, my madness deepens. It's getting harder to act like I don't understand the desperation and hunger that Daniel must have felt when he gave in to his desires.

God forgive me.

FOR MORE INFORMATION, questions, and upcoming works,
please follow the author at

https://www.facebook.com/EllisAurien/

CPSIA information can be obtained
at www.ICGtesting.com
Printed in the USA
FFHW020055081019
55414208-61180FF

9 781629 016665